THE KNEELING BUS

Beverly (Jones) Coyle is the co-editor of *Secretaries of the Moon*, the more recent of her two books on Wallace Stegner. She is a professor of English at Vassar College and lives with her husband in Greenwich Village. Born in Miami, she is a great-great-granddaughter of central Florida farmers.

THE KNEELING BUS

BEVERLY COYLE

PENGUIN BOOKS

PENGUIN BOOKS
Published by the Penguin Group
Viking Penguin, a division of Penguin Books USA Inc.,
375 Hudson Street, New York, New York 10014, U.S.A.
Penguin Books Ltd, 27 Wrights Lane, London W8 5TZ, England
Penguin Books Australia Ltd, Ringwood, Victoria, Australia
Penguin Books Canada Ltd, 10 Alcorn Avenue, Suite 300,
Toronto, Ontario, Canada M4V 3B2
Penguin Books (N.Z.) Ltd, 182–190 Wairau Road,
Auckland 10, New Zealand

Penguin Books Ltd, Registered Offices:
Harmondsworth, Middlesex, England

First published in the United States of America
by Ticknor & Fields 1990
Published in Penguin Books 1992

1 3 5 7 9 10 8 6 4 2

PUBLISHER'S NOTE
This is a work of fiction. Names, characters, places, and incidents
either are the product of the author's imagination or are used
fictitiously, and any resemblance to actual persons, living or
dead, events, or locales is entirely coincidental.

"Taking Martha with Me" previously appeared in *Grand Street*.

THE LIBRARY OF CONGRESS HAS CATALOGUED THE HARDCOVER AS FOLLOWS:
Coyle, Beverly.
The kneeling bus / Beverly Coyle.
p.   cm.
ISBN 0–89919–932–1 (hc.)
ISBN 0 14 01.4898 1 (pbk.)
I. Title.
PS3553.0947K58   1990
813.'54—dc20   89–20253

Printed in the United States of America

for

HENRY

ACKNOWLEDGMENTS

Three chapters in this novel were first brought to life by the editing of the novelist Brett Singer. Her students do not soon forget what she tries to teach them to hear in a sentence.

A special word of thanks to Ann Imbrie, Professor James Day, and the Reverend Doctor Norman Vincent Peale.

CONTENTS

TAKING MARTHA
WITH ME

My FATHER was a Methodist minister, but since he was never a strong "pulpit man," he rose quite slowly in the hierarchy of Southern Methodism. I grew up in large renovated parsonages all over rural Florida in the fifties. There were no religious pictures on the walls of those old furnished houses; my mother would not hear of it; my mother, Caroline, had been president of her sorority; my father was a liberal with advanced degrees who'd smoked cigarettes in the Navy. And I was taken to New York the summer I turned nine, where I saw Patty McCormack burn up her red shoes in *The Bad Seed*.

So it was a shock for me to learn that spring when I was still nine that my father was going to immerse a woman named Mrs. Mollengarden in the Atlantic Ocean at the Easter Sunrise Service.

My parents must have had reasonable conversations about it: how it actually came about that Mrs. Mollengarden had set her mind to a low-church ceremony; how Dad had already agreed to something so beyond his congregation's notion of good taste. Now they were breaking the news to my sister Jeanie and me, rehearsing their story for the larger fold.

"You're going to do it in the *ocean?*" Jeanie asked. Neither of us could quite grasp just how bad the situation was. There was still hope in the room for a simple sprinkling on dry ground.

But when my father didn't answer, we almost saw the whole thing and turned at once to look at Mother. Her lids fluttered bravely. "She has requested it," my mother explained. "Your father will take Mrs. Mollengarden out to the sandbar where the water is calm."

She might as well have said that he would take Mrs. Mollengarden out to the sandbar to be hanged by the neck until she was dead. We were better prepared to hand down that sentence to the woman ourselves than to be told that apparently all you had to do was ask for an immersion and it would be immediately granted unto you.

I thought of Martha, the Baptist preacher's daughter, whom I tortured occasionally in the neglected mango grove that separated her family's parsonage from ours. Martha was something of a dirty yard girl with impetigo below the knees. She had the habit of pulling out her eyelashes, and from time to time I was observed bossing her around the properties. I knew my sister disapproved of even the simple convenience of this connection, and I feared her indictment of me now that we'd been told of Mrs. Mollengarden. And so I was surprised when, after an early supper, Jeanie invited me to leave the house with her.

Jeanie could be counted on to sometimes love me in an emergency. We went to the town dump, where no children were supposed to go anymore since a man had exposed himself there to somebody in the high school.

My sister led me to a spot where she and her best friend, Celia, were planning to start a club. They had already cut windows in a refrigerator box and acquired orange crates. I knew I was never to come there again, but could sit inside for now if I was prepared to make fun of Mrs. Mollengarden, whom neither of us had ever met.

"She has big veins on one of her legs," I said. My kindlier self knew the woman was going to be merely doughy and hopeless, a woman without any make-up or good sense. But instead I invoked ugly details — crooked hips inside a sack dress, loose arms dangling down like monkey vine. Jeanie said none of it mattered; *she* wasn't going to the Easter Sunrise Service this year. No matter what.

I shifted my weight and thought about this challenge.

"I want to go," I admitted.

"So go," Jeanie said.

I looked at her. "I want to see how he'll do it."

"I'll show you how he'll do it, Carrie," and she grabbed me by my hair and pushed me under. I went down with a great gasp, screaming and laughing and kicking at the sides of the refrigerator box. ". . . in the name of the Father and the Son and John the Baptist," my sister said, "and when she comes up she'll be stinking . . ."

Jeanie didn't let go until she'd gotten in a terrific pull at the roots.

My father was out on the front lawn when I came up to report to him about Jeanie's clubhouse at the dump. He sighed and said we would all have to discuss this matter later, but for the moment did I want to come with him to Martha's house? He had asked Reverend Wenning if he could borrow a baptismal robe.

Of course I would come. I took up Dad's hand to lead him through the old mango grove. I was the only one in the family who had ever visited the Wennings on the other side, and besides the grove was full of hazards: old tires and tin cans and things I'd hauled in there myself. I made sure I led him over easy ground.

It was already twilight inside the big grove. The old trees had dropped blotched fruits of the day; mangos lay where they fell — split and exposed to flies. It was a freeze grove, and the still living trees were casting themselves away very slowly; they were dying in peace.

"Will you have her kneel down?" I asked. I steered him safely around the obstacles. He was making an effort to keep the deep, loose sand out of his shoes. I wouldn't have said anything in the world to hurt his feelings. I knew his family had been Assemblies of God, although it was not often mentioned, or them either. We had one photograph they'd taken of him in high-top shoes and a cotton dress with three starched flounces. He could have passed for some child on my mother's side, except that a detail in the picture gave everything away. There was no screen on the open window above my father's head.

"Dad! Will you have her kneel down?" I asked him softly.

"Who's that, sweetheart?" he said.

"Mrs. Mollengarden! When you get her out there will you have her kneel down or what?"

"Oh, I see what you mean," he said. "I suppose I could

do that. To tell you the truth I haven't thought about it."

"You could take a pitcher out there with you," I said. "You could have her kneel down and then pour water on her head out of the pitcher." I already knew which of my mother's would be appropriate. A plain buff one with no stripes.

"Ummm," he said, "perhaps I could." And then we fell silent and I seemed to see the invisible path in front of us — the one I'd heard about, the one you traveled if you were a big enough person. It lay as the strait and narrow under my feet.

We marched formally up to the back screen door of the Wennings' rundown parsonage, where Martha was watching out for us. My father had telephoned ahead, and Martha held open the door to let us in. Reverend Wenning had the robe right there ready in the dark kitchen. It was a well-used, very plain maroon robe with lead sinkers sewn into the hem. He pointed these out to us in an offhand way while my father slipped the whole thing on. Mrs. Wenning murmured that it was a good fit, averting her eyes to the floor, where the robe fell in plumb lines above the tops of his shoes.

"I suppose I could fix up one of our choir robes this way," Dad said. I heard one of the sinkers crack against his ankle bone.

Reverend Wenning was already saying it was no trouble to let Dad borrow this one. "You take it on with you, Preacher," he said. "This is an extra." Mrs. Wenning asked Martha to get a sack.

"Well, I appreciate it," Dad said. He made a point of taking the robe off as slowly as he could. Mrs. Wenning smiled and folded it carefully inside a brown bag from

Winn Dixie. We shuffled politely out the screen door to discover darkness had fallen over their back yard. Martha went barefoot a few steps with us beyond the porch stoop, then paused to watch until we came to the edge of the grove.

"Good-bye," my father called out. I was not sure what I heard in his voice — the unfamiliar neighborliness of it all; Reverend Wenning having the robe there in his kitchen like that. "Thank you!" he called.

The next day was Saturday and I found her watching for me from Habakkuk — the largest tree in the grove. She had all the trees named for books of the Old Testament. From this tree we could see the small road that ran past our houses and the two churches that sat three blocks apart. Even in daylight the grove was shaded and cool. But the sun had dried the fallen fruit and dispersed the heavy odors.

As I climbed to a favorite limb I'd staked out for myself, I was pleased to hear that Martha was curious about the robe. "You don't have a baptismal pool in your church," she said, though it was not a boast. Martha was not a swaggerer. The previous summer she'd grown quite bruised and yellow from a case of what they called mango poisoning. She and her brothers turned bright orange before it was over and they'd all had to stay out of the grove for months. I wondered that she never thought to brag about this episode in our uneventful days — a girl who'd been poisoned and lived.

I lay back on my limb and stretched my arms over my head. I had schemes for almost dying like that — going to the brink and returning safely. It was to be like a push from a swing — the seat brought up impossibly high and hurled with a snap to send me face up into the blue.

"My dad won't *need* a baptismal pool, Martha," I said.

I could rarely count on her to keep to the subject, even when she tried, as she did now after a little pause. "Do you want me to take you over to look at the pool in our church again?" Martha asked.

"No, thank you," I said, knowing she well remembered how I'd tricked her into letting me see their baptismal pool back behind the pulpit; we'd discovered it enclosed with a heavy curtain she said they tied to one side whenever there was a need. The sunken square was as dry as a culvert and had bounced our whispers around until we'd scared ourselves. I regretted my earlier interest in this facility now that immersion had come so legitimately and effortlessly into my own life.

"Don't forget, I'm getting baptized this summer," Martha said.

"I know," I said.

"Are you going to come? Did you ask your mom yet?"

"Yes."

I heard her sigh in contentment.

"But I can only come if you invite me, Martha. You have to send me an invitation."

"Why?"

"So that way my mom will know it's all right with your mom."

"My mom don't care."

I sat up. "Well, she has to care, Martha. Your mom has to care. Don't be so stupid."

Now, Martha was thoroughly confused and she looked off somewhere else with those frightening eyes of hers. My mother had told her she had such lovely eyes that she ought not to do that, pulling out her lashes like that. To me it was another exotic accomplishment completely wasted on her.

"My mom wants you to come," she finally said.

"Then all you have to do is send me an invitation."

"All right," Martha said. Of course she wasn't sure what it meant to send an invitation, and I knew that perfectly well. I saw her wipe her eyes with the back of her hand.

"Oh, now don't tune up and cry," I said. I climbed down off my limb and sat beside her on hers. "I'll tell you a secret if you won't tell anybody."

"I won't," Martha promised.

"Do you know why my dad borrowed your daddy's robe?"

"No," Martha whispered. "He don't know either."

"Because my dad is going to immerse a lady . . . in the *ocean*."

And I was aware at that moment I had said sacred words — words that were miraculously joined with deed. I saw myself taking Martha by the hand and guiding her into the safety of my father's denomination, where she could be baptized any way she wanted now, where she would eat right and fill out, where her hair would thicken and her color would improve and she would go to college.

"What's the matter?" I said when I turned to find that she'd pulled back from me, as if of all times in her life she would choose this one in which to press her advantage. But it was a look of helpless dismay. Poor Martha was seeing bathing suits and inner tubes; she was smelling hot dogs and suntan oil.

"You mean," she whispered, "he's going to do it at the *beach?*"

Sunday was Palm Sunday, the immersion a week away, and upstairs in the parsonage I poured powder in my shoes and watched the street filling up with cars. We Methodists had an oyster shell parking lot behind the new educational plant. But the Baptists just pulled up anywhere. From the bathroom window I could see Reverend Wenning's congregation parking, on grassy littorals, pickup trucks and station wagons. They stood around talking with Bibles pressed against their chests, calling out encouragements to their children, who shouted back at them from the trees in the grove. As a rule I never saw Martha on Sundays, but I wanted to find her that morning to show her something, to set her straight about the matter of the beach. I slipped out the back door and sneaked up unobserved to my edge of the grove, where I could watch for her. I had never done this before and knew instantly that Martha never had either. The mango trees were full of boys.

In church that morning, we all stood at the end of the service and sang an Easter hymn. A very tall man behind me bellowed out over my head and into the reds in the windows, which shone bright cherry. "Up from the grave He arose, / With a mighty triumph o'er His foes." I counted all the straw purses strewn in the pews in front of me. Somewhere in the church was a straw purse that belonged to Mrs. Mollengarden. It would be decorated in shell flowers with bits of wire stem like all the other ladies' purses, but it suddenly came to me that she was a very large woman, and that when my father took her in his arms, lowering her down, leaning over her, supporting her, rais-

ing her up again, surely — for there was no other possi-
bility — surely one of his arms, his *left* arm in fact, would
touch Mrs. Mollengarden's front. I rehearsed it all in a
large arena just inside my head. I stood hip-deep in early
April waters and silently curved my father's man's arms
around enormous spheres of space. There just wasn't a
question in my mind but that his left arm was going to
touch Mrs. Mollengarden's breast.

After church I told my mother in the kitchen that I thought
he ought to have her kneel down.

"I hardly think that's necessary," Mom said, thrusting a
set of napkins and silverware at me. She thought I was trying to dramatize the whole affair.

"But you see, if Mrs. Mollengarden would just kneel
down," I began, but my mother simply turned away, repeating that she thought such a thing would not be at all
necessary. She lowered her voice and whispered it. We
children were not to worry.

And yet when the Sunday meal began, as we all sat and
watched Dad carve up a roast chicken, my mother reasoned aloud. The air would be cold next Sunday morning,
she said, and after the immersion she wondered if he and
Mrs. Mollengarden wouldn't need to jump immediately
into the car and out of the wind, which would be coming
up fast with the tide change. She'd been thinking how he'd
need to have on something old and plenty warm under
Reverend Wenning's robe. No one would see because it
would be best if he simply arrived at the service wearing
the robe.

Jeanie sat and stared at the chicken. Dad arranged the
meat with some deliberation, as if he heard nothing. Every
time he lifted a little slice and delivered it to its proper spot,

the movement carried the easy suggestion that he was merely taking the bird apart and putting it back together again. My mother might as well have been speaking in tongues.

Well, there was no place to change except in the public bathhouse, she continued, and that was way up behind the dunes. No one would want to stand around waiting for him to change. If the air was unusually still there'd be sand flies.

"This looks delicious, doesn't it, girls?" my father said.

And we would have to remember to put towels in the car. None of us was to forget to remind her about the *towels*.

Had she let her imagination have full play, it would have probably involved that lovely Northern couple, Mr. and Mrs. Deaton, standing well dressed and dignified in the early morning light, watching Noel Willis, their favorite pastor, leading that large woman out to where Mom hoped the sandbar would be — not so far out so that nothing could be heard, but far enough to silhouette them demurely against the rising sun. Beyond that she could not go.

That afternoon I found my friend up in old Habakkuk.

"Get down," I said. "I want to show you something."

I waited with some impatience as she took special care to ease herself out of that tree, wipe her hands carefully on her print dress, then take from me the illustration I'd torn from one of my old Sunday school books. It showed John the Baptist standing beside Jesus in what was without question the *Sea* of Galilee.

"There you are, Martha," I said.

Martha studied it a long time; she was immediately in love with the illustration, and I saw her bite her bottom lip as she silently named for herself all the principals.

"You see? Even Jesus was baptized in the ocean."

Martha nodded her head. It was the River Jordan, she said, though she continued to nod that she took my point to heart. I saw then she'd never been my adversary in this matter of the beach. She'd simply had a fleeting image of the place as she knew it in Florida — ice cream wrappers poking up in the sand and very loud Yankees.

I pointed out to her some of the details of the illustration which interested me: John the Baptist stood somewhat behind Jesus and had his hands folded in prayer. The dove, descending from heaven inside a sun ray, dominated the scene, and, if one looked closely, it did look more as though Jesus had simply had water poured on his head. He didn't look especially wet.

"That's the Holy Ghost," she said, pointing to the dove.

"The Holy Spirit," I corrected her softly.

"Yes," Martha said.

"You can keep this," I said.

She blinked at me. "I got lots of pictures, but I don't have this here one."

"You keep it," I said.

"And you can have it back whenever you get lonesome for it," she said.

We were quiet for some time before I spoke again.

"Martha, when you get baptized this summer, are you going to kneel down in the water or what?"

"Grown-ups kneel down," she said. "Children stand up."

"Why is that?" I said. I was starting to feel better already. Martha had a way of looking far off to a place where things were supremely uncomplicated.

"I could find out from my daddy," she said.

"No, that's okay," I said. "I was just wondering."

Then Martha sat right down in the sandy grove and put the picture in her lap. I walked around behind her and leaned myself against a trunk.

"It's real quick, isn't it?" I said.

"What?" Martha said.

"Getting baptized. It doesn't take long, does it?"

"No," Martha said, "but it lasts forever."

She pushed her fine blond hair out of her eyes and turned to look at me. "You don't remember it, do you?" she suddenly said. "You was just a baby, wasn't you?"

"That's right." I looked her straight in the eye. "I was christened by a bishop."

Martha's eyes widened.

"You don't have bishops, do you?" I said, offhand.

"No!" she said. "What was he *like?*"

"He looked nice," I said.

"Did they take any pictures of you?"

She could not have done a nicer thing than ask to see photos. The Methodist ministers, posing in their creamy white suits, impressed Martha the most, I thought. Without my telling her, she saw that my christening had been an occasion. Those were district superintendents wearing the fashionable white suits of the day, and that was me in the white center, lying in the bishop's arms. I decided I could press her for more information while she studied the rest of the family album.

"And so when they kneel down, what happens then?"

Martha looked up. And I remember now how she must have looked, that Renaissance angels had no eyelashes. Michelangelo's Mary had no eyelashes. Martha could have been carved from pink marble. She got up slowly from the edge of my bed, knelt down on the floor, and crossed her arms over the front of her chest. Then she held her nose and leaned back as far as she could. Finally she pulled herself up and let her sweet breath out again. There was not a sound anywhere in the house. I could hear the waves flapping gently on the shore, and, while I knew everything would be all right, I knew they wouldn't be the same either.

"Martha?" I suddenly asked. "Do you want to come with us?"

"Where?"

"Do you think your mom would mind if you came next week to our Easter Sunrise Service?"

Martha blinked and looked far off.

"I'll ask her," she said.

I don't remember the long week that followed. I do remember sleeping rather lightly the night before in my blue-papered room down the hall from Jeanie, who'd wangled a sleep-over at Celia's so she could ride out to the sunrise service with Celia's family. Unfortunately, after the service Celia's family assumed Jeanie would return to town with us and we assumed she would return with them. And so, twenty minutes after my father had tried to immerse Mrs. Mollengarden in the Atlantic Ocean — all of us piling into the car to get them out of the knifing cold — Jeanie was left stranded at Boynton Beach. And when the poor child was finally rescued, she was in hysterics because she'd had no dime and had been afraid to ask a stranger for one.

My mother blamed it on all our confusion and worry. Things had been so eventful. My father and Mrs. Mollengarden had actually stepped in a hole on their way out to the sandbar. For a moment there, with only a few seagulls scolding and dipping frantically over the water, there had been no sign of them. Then a few moments later they had both come up again a bit farther out, where their feet found the edge of the sandbar which we'd always taken for granted, little children paddling out to it six days of the week. When we saw the two grown-ups standing tall at last, the water out there only came a little above their knees. Dad and Mrs. Mollengarden appeared merely to be wading in the sunrise. And so finally the ceremony had begun. No one was able to hear a word he said because people were still stunned at the near drowning they'd just witnessed before he could get the deed done and lead the woman, quite shaken, back to shore; whereupon my mother gave up all decorum and rushed to meet them with bundles of towels, which fell in the water everywhere as Dad searched around his feet in the vain hope that his glasses might have washed up somehow at that very point.

I was the only one who was not mortified by the interminable flailing moments before they reached the sandbar safely, and so fortunately remembered forever and ever exactly the way he did it. His right arm went around her shoulders as I had imagined and his left arm swung gracefully and firmly over Mrs. Mollengarden's large bosom as he lowered her down and said the words and raised her up again while Martha and I stood waiting with the small congregation. We held hands the whole time and Martha talked softly but a great deal, which I had not expected of her.

"This is right before the dove comes down," she said first of all when the two of them stood face to face and prepared to make that lovely embrace. And while Mrs. Mollengarden was under, Martha said amen and nudged me so that I said it too, quite involuntarily. But when they stepped silently apart there on the sandbar, and when they waded cautiously back to shore in light that scorched the waters, Martha told me frankly that she'd seen the Holy Spirit out there with them and that the Holy Spirit had kept them aloft.

THE
SEVENTH
DAY

THAT SUMMER I turned ten and bought a parakeet at Alma Turner's pet store in town. Before she started up the final transaction Miss Alma insisted on showing me a photograph of her granddaughter, Faybia.

"She looks like me," Alma said, leaning on her elbows, studying the likeness, "but I believe there's worse things in life." She held out a bleary photograph of a grown woman who I saw instantly would one day be me if I wasn't careful. The granddaughter looked to be forty, but was wearing a child's necklace on a blackened chain. A small gold cross was stuck in the middle of her throat.

"She lives up north," Alma said, reaching inside her bosom for a handkerchief trimmed with crochet. It was Florida in August and all the women in Boynton Beach had hankies.

Alma Turner was the most forward-thinking woman in our town. When her TV set — a mahogany Philco —

arrived from Miami, a photographer had rushed over to take a picture of Alma pointing a bony finger at the mysterious screen. I still had the clipping along with other special keepsakes — a lock of my own grandmother's hair and an abandoned collection of cigar rings from foreign countries.

Boynton Pets sold mostly tropical fish and kittens. Alma sold miniatures in the back as well — cups and saucers, teeny commodes, covered cake plates the size of acorns. Behind that was a set of rooms where she lived with a parrot she was willing to sell for fifty dollars. People thought she was kidding, but fifty dollars was a bargain, Alma said; she said folks around here knew nothing because they never traveled. She had taught the parrot to advertise. "I'm a bargain," the bird said.

"All the parakeets in this cage are my males," Alma explained. We stood in front of the special cages she'd made from chicken wire; the mesh tops sagged over branches strung on clothesline. "If you want yours to be a talker, you have to be sure to pick a male. They get a dark spot over their beak. It's the mark of intelligence."

Weeks before, she'd pointed out an ugly chartreuse lump of a bird who'd been hatched in July. I'd been in and out all month to see if the place above his beak would grow dark enough to distinguish him. Suddenly, in a matter of days, the spot had deepened to an ashy smudge.

"Yep, Carrie, he's going to be a real good one," she said, pleased for me. "When you get him home you spend some time now taking him on and off his perch. The trick is to put your finger in like this and let him walk right onto it before you lift him out."

My parakeet looked sideways and suspicious when she

offered him a step-up. But then, just as she'd known he would, he put a foot forward, my heart swelling at the thought of him doing that for me. I watched him swaying dangerously, trying to balance himself on his fragile chicken tongs. As Alma passed her hand in front of my face, he crouched as low as he could and hung on for the ride.

"How long will it take him to talk?"

"I don't make prophecies."

Alma deposited the bird inside the brand-new plastic cage that came free with the deal. As I carried him off, full of hope, she called out to me, "Just don't be asking for miracles."

The next day, a letter arrived from my grandmother. The envelope was so fat Grandma had used up a whole roll of tape to get the thing closed. I was in the mango grove behind our house, bent down over the cage, already coaxing my pet. "You silly bird, you silly Billy," I was saying over and over when Jeanie came out to break the news. "She's joined a Seventh-day Adventist church," Jeanie said. "Mom says they're more fundamentalist than anyone." My sister sighed wearily and knelt down beside me because she thought I wasn't listening, which was not the case. I felt sure something unusual was about to happen to our whole family this time, something I'd been waiting for.

Jeanie's voice went low. "They foot-wash," she said.

"They do not," I said.

"They do. They wash their feet right in the pews."

I closed my eyes and waited. "No they don't. You're making it up."

Jeanie shrugged her shoulders. "I'm telling you what's in

the letter. Go read it for yourself. If you *can* read. Mom and Dad are having a fight. Mom is crying right this minute."

Billy fluttered inside his cage and hopped to the perch nearest Jeanie. His head feathers sat straight up with pleasure when Jeanie made a few *tuck-tuck* sounds with her tongue; when she whistled, the kindness made him quite mad. He began nodding from the top of his cage to his toes, turning round and round on his perch, saluting her first high then low until he almost fell on his face.

"Your bird is as dumb as you are," she observed.

But I saw the real truth immediately. Billy would go to anyone.

My mother sat at the kitchen table, the letter spread out before her. I couldn't make out her expression. Dad leaned against the drainboard and watched me hang the plastic cage on a sturdy hook he'd put up in the corner.

"I certainly wouldn't have expected it," my mother was saying, expressing my thought almost at once. This thing had happened to her mother, but we all knew the dark weakness for fundamentalism came from Dad's side of the family.

The letter lay in two piles. Half of it was anchored with a saucer. Grandma had typed out every moment leading to her decision — the complicated details of her conversion. She'd used a two-toned ribbon so that words and whole sentences would stand out in red like the red words of Jesus in my Youth's New Testament.

I saw my mother thumb the pages and then give up. "Do they wash their feet in church?" I asked.

She looked at me. "It's just a ceremony, sweetheart."

I imagined all their feet exposed and a pile of socks and

shoes on the floor of some little brown church in the wood.

"What else do they do?" I said. (They would sing "Bringing in the Sheaves" for one thing.)

"Noel?" Mom said.

Dad took a pen from his shirt pocket and bided his time. He was a handsome man with a strong jaw who did nothing to set himself above his flock. Sundays and funerals, he stood naturally and gracefully as if he were standing on his own front porch. "It's their belief that we should worship on Saturday instead of Sunday," he said. "That's why they call themselves Seventh-day Adventists."

Mom stared at him as if she were having to take this in once more and just could not.

"But *Sunday* is the seventh day," I said, counting from my thumb, starting with Monday. I was a Monday's child.

Dad pointed to a calendar hanging by the phone. When I looked, all the Mondays in August had suddenly moved over. Four Sundays, at the head of each week and busy with penciled reminders, pushed everything down one. I saw, for the first time, that Saturday stood all by itself — extreme and final — as far away from us as it could get. Why had I never noticed this before?

Mom took my hand and turned away to look at Dad. "Mama's lonely. She's looking for a family with these people, don't you think? Noel?"

"Maybe you should invite her here."

Mom got up and put the letter in the sink. She hadn't intended this to be funny, but Dad gave a laugh, and it made my mother turn huffy.

"I have no idea what I should do," she said.

.   .   .

My grandmother wasn't lonely. None of us had ever seen her so pleased with herself. She said she'd talked to a lovely woman all the way down on the bus.

She began right off the bat. "It's one of the Commandments, darlin'," she explained. This was the simplest explanation for what she'd done, she said. "The seventh day is the Lord thy God's," she sang, lifting a pale pink corset from her suitcase and placing it flat in the top drawer of my dresser. I'd be staying in Jeanie's room, and I'd lined the drawers in gift wrap for Grandma — ironed Christmas paper with green and silver bells. "The seventh day is the Lord thy God's," she said.

There was a radiance in her face in spite of her fleshy nose and her wisps of dry fine hair. Mom came into the room with ice water. "Here we are!" she breezed.

The tray was too small; the glasses clinked sonorously together. Grandma patted my mother's arm. "Sunday is *not* the Sabbath day." She spoke in a new kind of voice, low and masculine. "Sunday is the wild solar holiday of pagan times."

There were things on the stove and Mother excused herself.

"They let the pagans keep their sun gods so they would convert easier. Maypoles, nakedness, graven images." Grandma clutched a gigantic brassiere in her arms. "They made Sunday into a false Sabbath."

"*Who* did?" I asked.

"They did it in order to fool the pagans," she said.

She sat on my bed and opened her notebook. She wrote the words "Sun God" and "Son of God" so I could see, she said, how the pagans might get confused and be accidentally converted. As she wrote, she moved her arm in a cool circular motion, her hand never touching the page. The fragrances of her were like all the summers of my life. I leaned against her powdered skin and studied the moles along her neck. Translucent, they hung by delicate threads.

"We must never be counted among their number," she said. "We must never be counted among those who changed the Law."

Downstairs Mother was getting the noon meal on. It wasn't like Grandma not to be down there helping — to be sitting instead with me in my blue-papered room. By now the casserole was on the table. Mom stood at the bottom of the stairs calling up to us. "Yoo-hoo!" she called. But Grandma seemed not to hear.

"We have proof they changed the Law," she continued, lowering her voice.

"Who *were* they?" I asked. "The pagans?"

"Oh, yoo-hoo!"

Grandma shifted to face me. This is why she'd come. She pressed my hand. ("Is anybody up there?") She whispered she had taken a long time figuring these things out. Hadn't it taken her all of her sixty-two years? She bent her big head to mine.

"Not the pagan, darlin'. It was the pope."

Mother walked around the table adjusting the forks. "Oh, there you are."

Grandma nodded at the birdcage in the corner. "What's his name, darlin'?" She was pleased for me.

"Billy." Jeanie moaned, as if there were no hope.

"Billy Billy?" Grandma called, and her voice had the familiar pitch and timbre he knew meant love. He acknowledged her with his practiced bows, the obsequious ups-and-downs of his long chest. When I opened the cage and let him step onto my finger, he flew straight to the top of her head, and she folded her arms slowly, pretending parakeets landed in her hair every day of the week.

"He has to go back to the pet store tomorrow to have his wings clipped," Mom explained, "now that he's used to us." She motioned that I should put Billy back in his cage, please. She looked at Dad. "Noel?"

We bowed our heads and Dad asked that the food be blessed to the nourishment of our bodies and us to His service. Grandma murmured an extra amen and we all relaxed.

The rest of the family sent their love. They were all fine — Carl, Grace, Aunt Dove, and Rita. But the freeze had done such dreadful damage. Carl and the boys were having to sell the fruit for concentrate this year.

"It's a shame," Dad said.

"And they're all upset with me, of course," Grandma said, patting Mom's arm. "Your aunt Dove says I've broken her heart." Grandma sighed. "She's hoping you'll talk me back to my senses."

My severe great-aunt Dove, with her deep-set waves of pearl-gray hair. I couldn't imagine anything that could upset her more.

"Well, we want to hear all about it," Mom said. She smiled at Dad, at Jeanie. At me. "Have some of the ham, Mother."

"Oh, no." She shook her head. "I don't eat pork, Caroline."

"Oh?" Mom said, staring at Dad for a moment. "I didn't realize."

"No pork and no coffee."

Later that afternoon, when she'd had her nap, I took her out to the mango grove. I'd pulled old wicker chairs out there by then. We sat down, and I got her to tell me what else the Seventh-day Adventists did. Well, they gave a tenth of all they earned; they refused liquor and stimulants. When she sat back, the late afternoon light cast leafy shadows on her face and arms. They never went to movies; they wore no jewelry; teenage girls didn't ever shave their legs.

Once in a while she leaned down to Billy's cage, repeating his name while he watched the brilliant, iridescent flies crawling in and out of his view. She told me how she feared the idea she might have died not knowing what she knew about the Sabbath. There would have been nothing worse than that.

"Do my parents know?"

"They don't know about the pope."

"Are you going to tell them?" I knew I wouldn't tell Mom if I were her.

Billy suddenly sang out something between a note and a word. Grandma took a stick and dug an old measuring spoon out of the sand. "It's my duty before I go."

When she said "go," I knew she meant her duty before she died. And yet I imagined it as a real journey, away from everything dear and familiar: the Methodist Church, her sister Dove, her children. Us.

For a moment I saw myself walking with Grandma along miles and miles of sandy road on a mission. Neither of us had a pocketbook.

The next morning, the wood shavings at Alma Turner's filled the air with a clean smell; her birdseed always made me think of spices from the Orient — caraway, cardamom, and anise.

And yet my grandmother didn't take to Miss Turner. When the two of us came into Boynton Pets, hauling Billy in his plastic cage, Alma asked a simple question Grandma refused to answer.

"Did you come on the train, Mrs. Jamieson?"

"No, I didn't," Grandma said, squaring off in front of the hamsters. And when it was clear she wasn't going to say how she came, Alma's hands fluttered to the back of her head to see if anything had come loose.

I blushed and had Billy walk onto my finger just the way she'd taught me. Alma smiled at my progress and let me know she was prepared to accept some people's ways. She was a business woman and had seen all kinds. We heard Grandma call out, "And what are *these?*"

"Why, those are True Gold guineas, Mrs. Jamieson."

"And you sell them to people?"

Alma gave me a sharp look. "Yes, ma'am," she answered, and, though she continued to stare at me, she removed a pair of scissors from under the cash register. She was an expert who, in an instant, had my parakeet spread out in her palm like a hand of glossy playing cards — the sharp edges of his wing repeating over and over a simple pattern of color. Until now I'd never seen these intricate shades. Someone had hidden them there — this ribbed and rigid array of unnamable greens.

Billy looked quite content before the blades began to come together and my grandmother had rushed to us. "Oh please. Please don't."

Alma met no one's eye when she put the scissors down on the counter and tapped her finger to make her point. If the Lord hadn't wanted us to have these birds as pets, she said, He wouldn't have given them the gift of human speech. She looked at me; wasn't she right?

"He hasn't said anything yet," I said.

And then Alma knew she'd been betrayed. She touched

a spring somewhere that collapsed my parakeet to the size of an onion bulb. I saw his smooth ball head pop out from under a thumb. He gave us all an encouraging chirp, but Alma thrust him back in his cage and handed me the whole shebang. "You said you weren't asking for a miracle."

"I'm not," I said. The exotic smells had suddenly made me lightheaded. Grandma had already left the store.

"Well," Alma said, pointing the scissors at me, "maybe you just *better*."

I found Grandma not far off, sitting on a bench in front of the post office. She was fanning herself with a piece of newspaper and breathing hard. The day was too warm and we'd walked too far. She said she had to be still for a minute. We sat together, watching the slow cars in town. I remember the Florida towns in that time well, so sleepy and ringing with no sound at all. Men and women lingered like drugged bees in the intense sun. You could sit and wait for an unlikely breeze to start up, high and out of reach, in the tops of the royal palms.

"It's such a long journey and I'm worn out," she finally said. "I should never have let myself get fat. It was wicked of me."

"Oh, Grandma," I said. I looked down at her swollen black shoes and studied the tiny perforations over the toes. We were in the Last Days, she murmured; that was certain.

"What will happen to you?" I said.

"The Lord will come for me in the clouds of heaven."

"Oh, Grandma." I hadn't meant to sigh, but I couldn't help it. I knew now why she'd broken my aunt Dove's heart.

·   ·   ·

After dark, after the family had gone to bed, I lay on the rollaway they'd set up in Jeanie's room, unable to sleep, imagining her journey. Once in a while I could hear Billy, ruffling the paraphernalia in his cage downstairs. Once, he sounded as if he were flying up to the blue-papered room where Grandma's whistles and rattles of breath took off like spirits out the windows.

And in the middle of the night I woke up thrashing, and Jeanie sat right up. "You want me to get Mom?"

"No," I said. I went into the hall and crept downstairs. I took Billy's cage and slipped out the back door despite his objections. His feathers had slicked down at the inconvenience of being jostled in the middle of the hot night.

Even in the dark, he recognized the mango grove, and, once settled there, he took in the drama of the tropics. He shook himself out and sidled up to his tin mirror to practice what he knew while I sat back in one of the wicker chairs and tried to imagine myself — grown, gone, and seriously counted. I'd be wearing a jungle helmet at the time I let myself be hurled into some latter day when I'd be old enough for courage.

For Africa.

My parakeet chirped and talked on to himself in the mirror and ignored me.

Africa was my push from the swing and into the wild blue yonder of all whooping confusions — "Red and Yellow, Black and White" we sang in the song about the children of the world. The fire dancing and grassy legs and the lawful bones in their noses. I began to hum. "They are precious in His sight . . . They are precious in His sight."

The next morning I went downstairs and confronted them before she woke up.

Mom folded her hands in her lap and waited for Dad to say something.

"It's true that the day was changed, Caroline," Dad finally told Mom. "It was done in the third century."

"Well, I never heard that before and I think it's all very interesting," Mom said, "but what matters is that we worship every week. Mama knows we believe in a Sabbath as much as she does."

"Why did they have to go and change the day?" I said.

"Who?"

"The Catholics."

"*Who?*"

"The pope."

Mom looked at Dad. "Do you know what this is all about?"

"One of the popes, I don't know which one," Dad said, smiling. "It's in the recordings of Eusebius."

"That's right," I said. "He changed the Ten Commandments." I raised my voice. "We should be worshiping on Saturday."

"Maybe we should be," Dad said. He winked at me as if we were in cahoots.

"Well," Mom said, "maybe he thought it was better to pick a day to distinguish Christians from the Jewish people. Saturday is *their* Sabbath."

(We knew about Jews the way we knew about Sir Isaac Newton. They were discoverers. They had discovered that God was One, and *no* one would have figured it out for a long time if it hadn't been for them.)

"Well, I wouldn't mind worshiping on the same day as the Jews," I said.

"Well, of course, I wouldn't either, sweetheart. My point is, back then people felt differently. It's important to try to appreciate why they might have thought it was all right to have a different day."

"They were trying to trick the pagans," I said.

"What?" Mom said.

I had always suspected she was gormless.

"Well, I certainly don't believe that anybody was trying to trick anybody," she said, getting up to put the milk away. "If we all go around thinking everything is a trick, where would that leave us?"

None of us had expected Billy to take that moment to speak — to say "Silly Billy" in the clearest of human voices.

"Listen to that!" Mom said.

And he'd even spoken with all the self-deprecation I'd been counting on, though I was in no mood to be pleased. Everything *is* a trick, I thought.

Out in the grove several days later, Grandma showed me something she'd pasted in her notebook. It was a color photograph of the pope, and I knew this was no good. If she was hoping to get them to listen, she would have to be more careful. She couldn't go showing a thing like that around the house — a color photograph of the pope clipped from *Life*.

"Now, then," she said, pulling her chair a little closer to mine. We were like girls doing homework, heads together, arms entwined. "I want you to look very closely at his crown. Tell me what you see."

On the pope's crown I could just make out the letters of VICARIVS.

"That means 'the substitute,'" Grandma said. Then she slowly turned over the picture to show me a Latin phrase she'd written in a white space on the back: VICARIVS FILII

DEI. She pointed to each word and read, " 'The Substitute for the Son of God.' "

Grandma and I had been reading Revelation for several days. There was nothing to match it in all of Methodism.

"I want you to write the mark of the Beast down at the bottom of this page. Then I'll show you something interesting that happens when we add up all the Roman numerals in the pope's title."

Right away I told her they would *never* add up to anything in the six hundreds!

"Maybe not," she murmured, "maybe not." But she began putting down letters anyway — just the I's and V's, etc.

V	5
I	1
C	100
I	1
V	5
I	1
L	50
I	1
I	1
D	500
I	1

"How did you get a *five* hundred?" I asked, startled.

"From the D, darlin'. From the D!"

My knowledge of Roman numerals did not extend to five hundred. I began to add the column expectantly, thinking how it was just like my teachers to leave me unequipped for anything serious. In a matter of minutes, when I began to bring down one perfect six, then a second, and, finally, a third, I gave myself over bodily to what had happened before my eyes. Three perfect sixes had shot up like cherries. I added the whole thing again to make absolutely sure.

Grandma tore the sheet from her notebook and gave it to me with a little flourish.

But by then I'd thrown myself against her, in love and astonishment.

Mother wept.

She hugged me against my will, saying she had to take back what she'd said the other day. This really *was* a trick, she said. Somebody had really been trying to trick Grandma. She pushed the paper away and put her head in her hands, exasperated. "Sweetheart, we don't believe in things like this. These are numbers. This is a coincidence."

I pulled the paper toward us and added up the column again. Already I'd adopted the urgent pencil scrawl of an adult. "This number is in the Bible!" I said.

Dad covered his mouth and got up from the table.

"I don't see what's so funny, Noel."

"I'm sorry, honey. I was thinking of something else."

"I wish you'd tell us what."

"I was remembering a few of the fellas in seminary. The more conservative boys used to talk about the Beast. It was surprising — the ideas some of those boys came up with."

"Well, I think it would be helpful if you'd tell us about that right now."

Dad hesitated. "This was during the war. Some of those boys worked out the numbers to explain Hitler. They found out Hitler's mother was born on the sixth of June in 1860. If you wrote it out GI style, you got six, six, six, zero, which was close enough for them."

Dad wrote down 6/6/60.

"I don't think that's very close," I said. "Besides, Hitler's dead."

"True."

"But that's not the point, is it, Noel?"

"No. It's not."

"Talk to her, Noel! Explain it to her."

"Okay, one edition of the *Communist Manifesto* had six hundred and sixty-six pages," Dad recalled. "That sort of thing."

I was getting mixed up. Mother had her head in her hands again, but now *she* was trying not to laugh.

"And don't tell us the Communists are dead," she said, letting go. "The Communists are everywhere."

I stared at her.

Dad pounded his fist. "That's right," he said, pointing his finger at my nose. "It may turn out to be the Communists. But before them it was probably the pope."

Mom sobered and lowered her voice. "Okay, enough," she said. "Let's not have anyone going around saying the pope is the Beast."

"The Whore of Babylon," my father whispered.

Outside the sun showed no mercy for the familiar objects simmering on our back stoop — Mom's frayed laundry basket, her dirty work shoes curling in the heat. I let the screen door slam shut on them. I'd made sure to let Mom and Dad see me take down Billy's cage and head off alone with him to the grove.

Mom rarely came out to the grove. Normally she stood at the edge peering in — oh, yoo-hoo. But in a few moments she had followed me and was entering from the far side, with her apron still on, her waist as narrow as a girl's. I began to squint at her — to squint at her slender feet sinking into the sand. I felt lean rancor come into my throat. By the time she reached me, I'd almost become, in the fifty yards from her kitchen to the trees, a Seventh-day Adventist.

"Dad didn't mean what he said about the pope," she said when she'd settled in one of the chairs. "You know that, don't you? He was joking."

Just the easy way she sat down had meaning for me now — the way she crossed her smooth, shaven legs at the ankle.

"We have respect for the Catholics," she said, "for all faiths."

"I don't," I said.

"Yes you do. Right now you're angry."

"I am *not*."

"Well then, I'm glad. Maybe we could talk about this." She unfolded the torn sheet from Grandma's notebook. For a moment Billy, uncertain of the bright paper, jumped around scolding the toys and little ornaments on the bottom of his cage. Mom waited until he was quiet again. "This *is* remarkable," she said, ironing out the paper slowly, then running a stub of pencil down the column of numbers. "But you know, Dad was just saying when he looked at this that the first word doesn't have two V's. The second V is really a U. *Vicarius*. It means vicar. Like the Episcopal ministers."

I watched dumbfounded as she gently crossed out the second V in the column.

"What are you doing?"

"There's no second V here, sweetheart. The Romans used to print their V's and U's exactly alike to make things easier when they engraved."

"Then why are you changing it?"

"I'm only trying to show you how some people can get numbers to work for them."

But everything was getting clearer and clearer. I was a witness to how someone like my own mother could take a pencil and change the Law.

"Pretty boy," Billy said.

On her Sabbath, Grandma stayed more or less alone up in the blue-papered room. Downstairs, while Billy preened himself on her shoulder, my mother sipped her coffee and alluded to a larger view of things.

"She's an older woman now," Mom whispered. "You, you'll grow up and go off on your own. To college, Dad and I hope, where you'll learn a lot of new things you've never thought about before."

When she stood up to make her journey to the icebox, to put the milk back where she always put it — just to the side of the orange juice — all the college photographs of her appeared in my mind. In her first yearbook, she'd started out as tiny as a postage stamp. And every twelve months after that they'd blown her up a bit bigger — to a calling-card size, to a shower invitation, to an extravagant full page of her own — my mother in a low-cut drape. An adjustment in the focusing had turned her into everybody's dream girl.

"I'm not going to college," I said. "I'm going to do something you'd never think of in a million years."

I would have given a good deal for the courage to walk to the icebox and pour the whole bottle of milk over my head.

"You can do whatever you want to do; that's my point," Mom said.

I spun around in the direction of Africa. I saw my own dad standing on the other side of our screen door, squirting the family car with a hose. For a second I imagined he was trying to put out flames. "In a trillion years," I said, jerking around again and startling Billy into flight. He alighted on the screen door, then craned his head around to look forlornly back at me the very moment Dad bounded onto the stoop to tell us something, opening the door wide and flinging Billy's two or three ounces into the air.

"Whoa!" Dad shivered as if some invisible soul had passed right through him. Mom gave out a cry and Jeanie ran in from the living room, thinking someone had gotten burned on the stove. By the time Dad recovered, a little furious at his own part in the accident, he was accusing us all of carelessness and stupidity. His anger fell on Jeanie, who burst into tears, saying she didn't even know what he was talking about.

"Something made Billy fly to the screen, Noel," Mom explained. But she was as upset as he was. "It's no one's fault. He's never done that before."

Dad turned and ran into the yard. "Well, that's just great!" he shouted back at us. "And now he's gone."

I ran upstairs to my room, not expecting to find Grandma dozing, not hearing anything. Meanwhile under my feet things were already calming down to Dad's deep drones and Mom and Jeanie's quiet reconstruction of what had happened. For a moment, I stared out a window, blinded by the afterimage — Billy's green wings blackened in the sunlight. I thought I heard the delayed report of the snap he'd made, vanishing without me into the world.

I shook Grandma's arm. "Billy flew away," I said.

"Oh, dear," she said, sitting up and taking my hand. She had fallen asleep reading, still dressed in her thin nightgown because of the heat.

But she was listening to them below. "You should go back down there," she said. "They're upset."

I sat beside her on the bed. "No, they aren't."

"Yes, they are," she said. "I'll get dressed. Go tell your mother everything's all right. She's all upset down there."

When I turned in the doorway, she was kneeling in her thin gown. She hid her big nose in her hands and let the tangled wisps of her head fall low. I didn't want to look at the enormous flesh on her upper arm as she knelt alone at the side of my bed. Her arms pressed oddly against her breasts; the bare bottoms of her feet appeared swollen and shapeless. I hurried away, embarrassed, and found Mom sitting by herself at the kitchen table.

"Carrie, we're so sorry," she said.

None of them had closed the screen door. It stood open as if they thought there was no point in closing it again. He'd so completely flown the coop.

"I'm going out to look for him," I said. "Grandma's praying."

"Oh, sweetheart," Mom said, the defeated sigh in her voice too familiar for me to bear.

I took down the cage above her head, lowering it slowly until she and the table slid to the other side of a deep divide that must always be there now. My life would start from the opposite edge, and as I left the house with Billy's cage I finally asked for a miracle.

Please let me find him, I said when I looked over my shoulder and saw Mom following me out the screen door in her black high heels. I took a good look at her standing there, slender and lovely in the yard, looking up at the window of the papered room. I heard myself offer up a silent deal, a real bargain: If He'd just let me find Billy, if He'd let me bring him back and put him down before her very eyes, I'd go and *do* something. I saw myself rattling along with an empty cage — rattling myself down the highway and right out of town and on my way — when what really happened was that I nearly stepped on that almost invisible chartreuse onion bulb, about five minutes later, out in the mango grove, which was as far as Billy or I managed to go.

I put out my finger and watched him climb up, one chicken foot and then the other. In all that time, he'd been poking around beneath the trees — that silly bird, that talker — scaring the brilliant flies.

And I wondered, suddenly, what I would do without my wicker chairs, or the box of cigar rings and the trees and all of Boynton Beach. They hung like miniatures above the funnel that would suck them to the bottom of everything. If He'd just let me find him, I'd prayed, if He'd let me bring him back and put him down before her very eyes, I'd go ahead and believe He was real and coming soon, out of the blue, to take me from her and break her heart.

FULL OF
BEANS

BOYNTON BEACH is part of Florida's Gold Coast now — a string of million-dollar golf courses with sand-traps shaped like pearls. But it was a farmer's Boynton I knew in that early, oddly godly time of my life. When I was ten, God's presence came and went like an undertow to which I felt I'd never succumb, despite the efforts of my grandmother. I was too Methodist and I was not religious. There'd be some action I'd have to take if I was going to be found religious instead of fake. There'd be a gesture — some dangerous leap from my safe peninsula. And whenever I wanted to test myself, to see if my position had changed, I would simply ask, in secret, whether I was ready now to give myself over. And the answer was always no, that I was not, that maybe I would be later but probably not then either.

Not because I wanted riches or clothes.

What I wanted to be sure of was a husband.

When I searched my soul, I found a husband every time. Sometimes God seemed to be there waiting and worried; but usually the still small voice I heard was that of a dark-haired husband speaking in my mind and heart. For as long as I could remember, I'd heard him. He had the voice of a radio announcer.

And so I knew the image of myself on a steamboat down a muddy river in Africa could not be me.

It was not possible. Not unless the husband turned out to be a Doctor Schweitzer or Tom Dooley or Peter Marshall.

Boynton's Ocean Boulevard was a strip of tar when the first glittery celebrities swooped in from Miami to buy up our beaches. The newcomers built invisible mansions behind the sand dunes and dug tunnels under the highway so that they could walk straight to the water without being seen by trucks hauling hydroponic tomatoes between Boynton and Delray. The natives in town liked to think of them, slinking back and forth out there under the boulevard. By 1953 unknowing cars sped over a celebrity tunnel every two hundred feet. There were few landmarks. We could see Gail Patrick's widow's walk from the road. When my mother's sister visited us again, my flat-chested cousins sporting high-riding ponytails, Boynton Beach was the winter home of the Linelle Sisters. We took our guests sightseeing after church. We had something to show them, we said, driving them slowly down Ocean Boulevard until we saw the thick hedge of punk tree and stopped the car. Behind that shrubbery? we pointed. Behind where the high ladder stuck up on the other side? That was the winter home of the man who found the Dead Sea Scrolls.

.   .   .

Early that summer our street got a special kind of celebrity all its own — Everett Garrison, the new police chief — imported, we assumed, from another and bigger Florida town. My father was imported, and we were due to move to a bigger place ourselves soon. In my mind Dad's stock went up when the police chief bought the only other house on the block that looked like our parsonage — the last of the two-story affairs with cupcake coatings of bright peaked stucco. The vintage pieces sat facing each other in a standoff.

Until the chief bought it, the house had been rented to a World War I pensioner who set out empty whiskey bottles along the curb for pickup. An old naval officer, he always called them his "dead men."

Suddenly he was dead himself.

The paper boy had looked in a window and seen the old hero lying there on the double bed, where he'd been at rest for two days.

School was out, and I got to witness the sudden activity — Everett Garrison, in his holster belt, arriving with an ambulance and a lot of scrawny men a great deal younger than their boss. I knew a few of the officers from our church. They had wives and small children flanking them on Sundays, but in the yard across the street they trailed like baby quail after Everett while he made his routine investigation. Everett Garrison had full silver hair and a wonderful back and legs he planted three feet apart as if, while he waited, all good things would roll to those feet and just stop. He stood over the officers, watchful, when they sat together on the porch stoop, sharing the coffee from a silver thermos. Weeks later we heard he'd bought the house from

someone up north. Soon his men, dressed in dungarees —
boisterous and full of beans — were moving their chief in.
I saw them carry the heavy furniture wrapped in quilts and
surplus blankets. The first thing of a personal nature the
neighborhood knew of Everett Garrison was that he had a
wife, after all, as well as a lot of new blond furniture.

It was crushing to learn about the wife after seeing Everett Garrison, glamorous behind sunglasses, in the yard
across the road. I found myself waking up in the middle of
the night, wondering what he kept inside those leather
pouches sewn into his holster belt. His squad car gave off
a high-pitched sound inaudible to the other members of
my family.

I'd rise and look out my window at all hours. I had been
given my first pair of baby-doll pajamas that summer, and
the two exciting things about waking up in the middle of
the night were Everett's squad car out there in front of the
house and myself in a diaphanous shorty top with real
"spaghetti" straps.

The wife was too old for Everett, it seemed to me. She
was in her forties, my mother guessed — the same age as
Everett. Mom called her "handsome." She was a little
overweight, but very smartly dressed and haughty. Or
perhaps shy, my mother said. At first she refused to look
our way when she came out of her house. She waved to us
only when Mom left her no other choice. We'd see her
walking to her car in tailored suits and expensive shoes and
always carrying a pastel hatbox. It could be ninety degrees
and the sun overhead, but Mrs. Garrison would come out
in one of those linen capes that we saw in fashion magazines at the time. My mother had sewn herself a red one on
her own machine.

"Hello, Elaine," my mother called one hot morning. Mrs. Garrison slammed the trunk and waved with her back turned to us. Behind the glare of the car window her face appeared veiled and featureless, and it was that same afternoon I began my delirious spying.

Everett never came outside to move sprinklers around or spray bug poison under his house. Instead he brought out magazines — black-and-white pictures of yachts and sailboats crowding the pages — and plunked himself down in one of the heavy lawn chairs someone had painted gunboat gray. If Martha Wenning was around, she and I would step straight into his view and strut about in the road with our dolls. The first time he spoke to us, he called out to Martha, asking her if she knew how to tack.

The two of us took several strides into his yard. "I don't know what that is," Martha said.

When Everett laughed, he hooted. He reminded me of that actor from *Carry on Sergeant* with the exaggerated veins in his arms. He pushed back a red-billed cap and looked at me, taking his rolled-up magazine and swatting at my legs. "Go on in there and close the door." Incredibly, he was waving us into his house. "Go on! I'm trying something out. I want you to listen to something for me." He looked impatient for a moment and then spoke warmly. "It's okay. Pretend it's the middle of the night."

Martha followed me in without a word. Mrs. Garrison wasn't home, but we stopped just inside her foyer when Everett closed the door behind us. For a whole minute we stood, transfixed, in front of the library table we'd seen from the yard. Lying across the table was Everett's enormous belt with all the molded leather pouches. The gun part was the least of it. I reached out and ran my hand over the compartments — the many different flaps with gold snaps big enough to reflect my pursed lips. Along with the belt there was a collection of figurines — ceramic maids of a mysterious purpose, wearing gowns and carrying gauze parasols, some reading books with the print painted on as gold lines. My mother had learned to paint china as a girl. The hopeful expressions on their faces had been accomplished, I knew, with a mink brush whose tip was one single hair. Martha moved closer to me. I could hear the two of us breathing. Everett suddenly took hold of the heavy doorknob outside and shook it as hard as he could. What I was hearing was the sound a man would make if he wanted to get into the house and start stabbing everyone in sight.

On Sunday I studied the backs of men's heads and listened to the long text on the Wise and Foolish Virgins, carrying brass lamps for the Bridegroom. Some lacked extra oil for their vigil. I pictured distinguished-looking teenage girls in a courtyard, drifting into two groups. Ten wise virgins to one side were smiling sadly, and ten foolish virgins to the other side were rocked with uncontrollable giggling. "You do not know what hour He cometh," the lay reader read. "He is like the thief who comes in the night." I looked over at Nadine, who sometimes passed me notes she scribbled inside the church bulletin. Nadine was well on her way to being one of the foolish virgins. She made her o's into little hearts and dotted her i's with stars. "Isn't th♡s b♡r♡ng?" all her notes began.

It was a slow hour of the same people and the same backs

of heads, nothing much changing. But I was never bored. It was always hot. As I drowsed, I was thinking how people were young and old at the same time; a few were balding early and worked for Everett Garrison, who did not go to church, while in an ancient time two dozen virgins stood in a stone courtyard trimming lamps for a vigil. These were fine-spun intuitions of the now and the then squeezed to a scene, observed through a pinhole. I was both here and there at once.

"S♡ l♡ng!" all her notes ended.

Two days later, the text from Sunday figured in the ordinary world and I was rewarded: a thief climbed in a window at the Aubrey house on Keanway Road, where Mrs. Aubrey was giving a bridge party.

More startling was Everett's mention of it to Martha and me the next morning; otherwise we might not have ever known of such a thing or that the man was thought to be pulling this little job all over the area. At ladies' parties. He would go in the window where the pocketbooks were nestled on the bed and at no time would the women chatting in the living room hear a sound.

"He takes the wallets out of the big bags and slings the little bags right around his neck." Everett reached over and tousled the top of Martha's head. "The next time he does it, I'm going to be right there when he comes out that window." Everett turned around in his chair and looked at his own house. He pushed his hat back. "What do you think, Martha? You like parties?"

That day Martha's sundress was hanging loose around her skinny middle, and it irritated me something bad that we were getting glimpses of her navel.

"Were the ladies playing cards?"

Everett had forgotten Martha was a Baptist. He got up and gave a hoot. "I'm afraid they were, Martha! Woo-wee, I'm afraid they were." He bounded through his front door and disappeared into the hall. We heard him, still hooting, as he made his way to the back of his house. I'd never felt so embarrassed for anyone in my life.

"He didn't mean to be mean," I said. Martha wouldn't look at me.

"Hey, I saw a bridge party one time," I said.

I told her how all the ladies' cars had attracted my attention from a block away. I'd hidden behind the cool waxed hoods, and watched them play and fan themselves and eat things with their fingers. The hostess hadn't bothered drawing the drapes. When they stood up to enter the kitchen, the windows framed them from shoulder to thigh — sculpted, busty torsos of women in print dresses and hard white beads.

"He didn't mean to be mean," I said.

"Do *you* believe in cards?" she said.

I was dangerously inspired. "Martha," I said, "I saw all their pocketbooks in the bedroom."

She looked to see if I was lying.

The pocketbooks I'd seen belonged to women who'd come to my mother's social. They'd put them on my parents' bed for the evening, and I'd gone through practically all of them — freeing the loose mints from silk compartments, dabbing on oily perfumes, peeling open cigarettes, reading messages on curled pieces of paper. I told Martha about a scarf I'd found with pills tied up in it, and a crocheted bookmark in the shape of a cross. One woman had the Gospel of Mark in a little pamphlet the size of a checkbook.

Martha nodded. By now, she said, the thief would have a lot of stuff like that in his house.

I said he only had an apartment probably. Martha didn't know what an apartment was until I explained. Then together we added things to the list: a suitcase full of sample lipsticks the size of toy bullets, tiny sewing kits, and flat boxes of Sen-Sen.

We knew he'd have red wallets with pictures of movie stars and husbands inside. My own wallet was fat now. It was the style, and I'd stashed it with interesting printed sayings or jokes that could be passed from girl to girl down a pew. I had a calling card that said:

> Knock Knock.
> Who's there?
> Good.
> Good who?

The other side said GOODRICH TIRES. Nadine had spent devotional minutes on it one Sunday, turning it slowly in her palm before writing across the face of the bulletin, across the face of the Good Shepherd, "Where did you *get* it?"

"Martha!" I said. She was startled to attention.

"What?"

For a moment I couldn't think what I wanted to say about the plenty of it all — objects spilling and multiplying. Loaves and fishes. Everett telling us things, letting us in on what he knew.

I took her arm and led her out of his yard. We went into the road and leaned against his squad car. The light on top suddenly seemed as big as a lampshade.

"What?" she whispered. Maybe she was in love with him too. Our situation was doubly hopeless.

"Everett is having trouble with his wife."

"He is?" she said.

I thought of Mrs. Garrison's library table — of the girls pretending to read as they gave each other secret looks. "He wants to divorce her," I said, "now that the children are grown."

"How many children did she have?" Martha said.

I shrugged. "She never had any," I said.

"Then where's she going to live?" Martha said.

"In Miami," I said.

Later that evening Everett Garrison walked in on my family unannounced. He walked through the front door as if he were coming up from a celebrity tunnel under Ocean Boulevard. He smiled at me as if he knew to the inch my intolerable confusion at seeing him.

It was nice of him to stop in, Dad said. Well, Everett said, he'd been meaning to come over all along. He had a pan of fresh grouper and was inviting himself to supper if that was all right. Everyone sounded a little flabbergasted and delighted. Oh, of course it was all right, come on back to the kitchen.

"My wife's in Miami," Everett said.

"Well, where did you get this beautiful fish?" said Mom.

I stood in the doorway watching Everett insist on doing the fish himself, my mother demurring, Dad and Jeanie grinning when he tied on an apron and anchored himself in front of the stove. No one knew how to act. Dad sat on the countertop and passed a jar of olives. Mom asked about that doorknob jiggler who'd been scaring everyone — jiggling their doorknobs, then fleeing into the night.

"Do you suppose it's the same man?" Everett said, turning to look at me.

"The same man as who?" Dad said.

"It was an easy job, going in the window like that," Everett said, ignoring the adults. "How long do you think it'll be before he finds another party?"

"Who?" Dad said.

"I bet he looks for cars parked out front. What do you bet?" Everett said, winking at me. By now I was blushing.

"What are we talking about?" Dad laughed.

In telling the details of the party robberies, Everett got serious. He knew it might sound unusual, but he wanted Mom and Dad to know he was having a stake-out party at his own house, day after tomorrow. The guy obviously went around looking for women's groups, and some of his boys thought if they came dressed up in dresses they might get lucky.

Jeanie looked at me; she was crushed. She was due to leave for camp the next day and would miss the whole thing. We'd heard tales of men dressing up for the Lions Club — widely rumored fashion shows in which men teetered around in heels and put on large weddings in their wives' formals. Old chiffon and taffeta.

They might get lucky, Everett went on. At the very least he thought we should know what was going on over there. He wanted to have the party while his wife was out of town.

"Well, you don't really expect to catch him, do you?" Mom said. "Do you think it *is* the same person?"

"We just don't know yet," Everett said. "But if the man is still in the area, we know he looks for a lot of cars and a house full of women. My men are going to bring over all the pocketbooks they can find."

The whole thing caused a tremendous argument later on between Jeanie and Dad. Dad had to promise Jeanie that I probably wouldn't be allowed to stay home to watch Everett's party. We probably would all go somewhere else for the evening, Dad said. Maybe over to Nadine's house.

Jeanie finally calmed down and let him help her finish packing. "I'm taking these tops," she yelled to me at one point. When I didn't answer, she yelled down the hall, "Hey, I'm not kidding, you'd better come in here and see what I'm taking!"

I had wandered into the bathroom, where my mother was putting on cold cream. I was feeling funny now because of the things I'd said about Mrs. Garrison. I had a brief fear of the woman opening her suitcase in Miami and finding her figurines there, all broken. The idea made my teeth chalky. I asked Mom if she thought Everett was going to divorce her. It was the closest thing I could manage in the way of a confession.

She said she didn't know who I'd been talking to, but she'd like to know where girls got their ideas. She looked down where I sat on the rim of the tub. I heard her sigh as she turned her face to the mirror. There was one thing she didn't like besides a thief, she said, and that was a snoop.

The real show, the one Jeanie thought she would miss, took place the next morning before she'd left for camp. Mrs. Garrison came back from Miami, or wherever it was she'd gone, in time to meet an enormous Mayflower moving van in the middle of the street. The van threw our whole house in its shade for most of the morning. On the side of the truck a white ship sat on top of four blue waves, and when it was gone, the windows on the front of Everett's house reflected back our house and a blank sky. Mrs. Garrison had not even thought to leave him the drapes. Mom didn't know what to say to me in the woman's defense. But, then, she didn't have much experience with divorce. Mrs. Garrison had made it look like a caper.

"Where will she live?" I asked.

"Sweetheart, I haven't the slightest idea," Mom said. "You seem to have more information about her than anyone."

All I could do was move my arms and shrug. I was getting cold feet.

But at noon the neighbor lady driving Jeanie's group to camp showed up and asked us the very same thing. Mrs. Gregg really was a snoop, well known, and had heard about the moving van in town at the post office, where people said Mrs. Garrison had a private mailbox. Mrs. Gregg slowly pronounced the woman's unusual maiden name for us and rolled her eyes. That *name* explained a lot, she said. "I heard she has her own penthouse in Miami."

I didn't know what a penthouse was. I ran upstairs to ask Jeanie, who'd been sent back for her medicine.

"It's a jail, moron head," Jeanie said, shining her new flashlight in my face.

"A *penthouse?* Are you sure?"

"Uh-huh," she said. "It's for gangsters and moron heads. Like you."

·   ·   ·

Everett didn't return all day. In the afternoon I pretended to be ill and stayed in bed upstairs under the chenille spread, watching his empty house. I held ice cubes in my mouth to mortify the flesh. Had they been hot coals I would have folded them in my tongue or swallowed them down whole to let them burn up my heart.

I wondered what I had the power to undo. At the movies, when the picture ran backward, making us all laugh, a woman on the hot tracks could be bounced back into willing arms. And if I could have bounced Mrs. Garrison back, I would have done it. I would have made her into an India rubber ball.

"She's upstairs resting, Martha," I heard my mother explain. "Why don't you come outside and help me hang these up?"

I watched Martha take my place at the dilapidated clothesline. I could hear Mom putting long questions to her. Martha answered in shy sentences, handing over the clothespins one by one. The lilt in their conversation, the friendly music of my mother's voice, seemed to come from some meadow portrayed in one of those religious books for young people she didn't in her heart approve of. But now I would gladly have taken the meadow and the two of them in it. I wondered whether I might not put everything back in place if I were willing to push out the screen and dive with true faith into my mother's basket of sheets.

When Everett came home in the evening, he went inside his house and then came right back out to take in the lawn chairs. His movements were quick and energetic and full of courage. Carry on Sergeant. He snapped shut the chairs as if they were branches he could have broken over his heavy thigh. And I realized then, remembering the moving van which seemed days ago, that he had nothing left inside the house now — only those chairs to sit on. Only his plans. Only me.

After dark, the ceiling lights came on in every room of Everett's house. A low wattage that made his blank walls look yellow. Candlelit.

"That's eerie," Mom said. Dad said he thought he ought to go over there and talk to him. And in minutes Mom and I could see the two of them walking around together through the empty house. Everett was wearing his cap.

"Well," Dad reported on his return, after some probing, "I guess he's all right. He said the thief will be able to see in better now. Without the drapes."

"That's doesn't sound all right to me," Mom said.

When we looked again we could see him go into his little bathroom. He seemed to be trimming his hair into the sink. "He should put up sheets in the meantime," Mom said. Later she came into my room and found me still watching.

"He's changing the light bulbs," I said. "I hate this," I suddenly told her.

Mom looked and saw that the whole house was outrageously bright now. He'd put 200-watt bulbs in every ceiling fixture. She made me lie down. She was terribly sorry for the Garrisons, she said, but this had nothing to do with me; we were all from different walks of life. "Whatever happened over there has been going on a long time."

Once they were in bed, I heard Mom ask Dad if someone shouldn't try to find out where Mrs. Garrison was. She meant *he* should find out, though the Garrisons weren't members of our church. I stood in the hall in my spaghetti straps, wondering for the first time in my life what in the world it was my father did for a living. He visited people.

"You might be able to find out something we can tell Carrie," Mom said. "She's upset about this. Didn't Everett tell you anything?"

But by this time they thought they heard me creeping around outside their door.

"Good night!' my father called.

The next day when I asked her, my mother closed her eyes and said she didn't know if we would stay home or go out for the evening. She assumed I wanted to watch the party from our house, which was not the case. I didn't want to watch it at all.

"Dad and I will have to decide later," she said. Someone was knocking at our front door.

We found Mrs. Gregg standing there, pretending to have stopped by to report on Jeanie's cabin assignment. Mrs. Gregg had helped the girls settle in; she talked about cubbyholes and name tapes for a while. But soon enough she got to the police chief's wife and her moving back down to Miami, which, Mrs. Gregg said, was where Mrs. Garrison probably came from in the first place. Mrs. Gregg said she'd lived down there herself for a while when they were taking the fifties census. Mrs. Gregg lowered her whole head and began to murmur with her lips closed. She never wanted to go there again.

"We had Meyrowitzes on one side and Abramowitzes on the other, and when I gave the census taker my name that poor man looked at me and said, 'Lady, I could just *hug* you!' " Mrs. Gregg laughed and sighed and repeated the tone she remembered so well — that poor man's utter relief: he could just have *hugged* her.

Mom said she thought she heard the phone.

But, Mrs. Gregg went on, hearing there was no phone, turning the whole thing in a different direction, lowering her voice, tightening her jaw: she'd heard Elaine Garrison was plum in the middle of a nervous breakdown. To have taken all their furniture like that? Mrs. Gregg sighed. Lord, she said, it's where it all led, didn't it?

Mom said she wasn't sure what she meant.

"Now I guess we're supposed to act like nothing happened," Mrs. Gregg went on. "We can't even take him over a casserole or a meat loaf. Not in *these* times." Mrs. Gregg looked right at me then. "Honey, the man would think we had our eye on him."

I knew of one nervous breakdown. Mrs. Willey's. When people talked about Mrs. Willey picking up the pieces, I'd always imagined her on a beach picking up little shells.

Would she have felt the difference if I'd been nicer to her, last winter when the adult and youth choirs combined for three Sundays and I'd stood beside Mrs. Willey in the women's section, silently condemning her turkey wattle?

I was sure she hadn't known unless some women knew everything.

Martha came over in the afternoon, and Mom sent her to my room.

"Go on up there, Martha. Get her outside playing. Do you ever mope yourself, Martha?"

"No, ma'am," Martha said.

She stood beside me and watched the men below unloading card tables and chairs from a pickup. But I wasn't going to have her stand there and privately judge them.

"Men don't play bridge," I said. "They're just going to wear dresses and pretend to be at a bridge party." I told her of the special bed they'd made up in the darkened room at the end of the hall. Dad and I had gone over with some food for him and he'd taken us back there. The pocketbooks would lie heaped in an inviting, loose array. They were going to extend a few threads down the hall to the living room. All anyone had to do was touch something on the other end of the threads and two white tissues would leap across the floor. When *that* happened, everyone would continue to chat while Everett slipped out the back; two more out the front. They'd be at the window to catch him coming out.

Martha didn't say anything at first. Finally she said she guessed they'd play poker.

I didn't know what poker was.

"Men's cards," she said. She rested her elbows on the sill. "The thief won't know the difference."

When they'd taken in the tables and chairs, the men stood out on the lawn, smoking and horsing around. One of them suddenly put oranges inside his T-shirt to make himself pointy.

"Look," Martha whispered, slapping her hand on her heart. I felt the same bad little jolt of shame and didn't know how to defend them now.

But everyone was telling him to cut it out. They threw the oranges around the yard for a while before they piled, whooping, into the pickup and drove away. We saw Everett flopping down on his steps to thumb a magazine. This gave me exactly one last minute in which to look at him, alone, before my friend dropped the cannonball.

"Some time he'll marry another wife," she mused.

"What do *you* know?" I said. "You don't *know*."

"Everybody does when they get divorced," she said.

"Not right away," I said. "Not right away, they don't."

"No," Martha said, "not right away."

The ladies began arriving in twos.

Mom and Dad and I had barely sat down to a late supper. First we heard the gravel crunching under the heavy wheels. Something about the way the doors began opening and slamming shut made me know they were going to look like real women. They opened the doors the way women did arriving anywhere — all the slamming and reslamming. When we heard the laughter we went to our windows, where we were forced to see my version of the wise and foolish virgins — over a dozen men, dividing themselves into groups, cavorting and gossiping on Everett's lawn. They shifted their large pocketbooks occasionally and tossed their stiff tight curls. Those without wigs wore hats and seemed less forthcoming. But from the slothful stances we could see how proud they all were of the common achievement: the belted waists and rounded hips, the shapely calves. A thief wouldn't be able to tell the difference between them and real women unless he looked closely. But if he did, he would see the busts were too similar.

Behind them the house appeared to have furniture in it. Everett had put bouquets of plastic flowers around in the front rooms. Mom said the bouquets looked as if they might be sitting on crates. Come on, she said; she wanted us to finish supper before it got cold.

"All right," Dad said. But we couldn't pull ourselves away. And the men, too, seemed reluctant to go inside. They stood in the yard, admiring themselves, their voices jumping from little purrs to high whoops of joy. When they modeled, they all swung their pocketbooks high.

Everett came to his door — the only shoulder-length blonde on the scene, and I heard my mother sigh. The ladies sent up a frightening, high shout to their leader, who'd been so much more daring than they. "Doris," they called as they made their way to him. Everett was wearing an outrageous sundress, which exposed his alarming, indissoluble flesh.

He'd done something to himself that was not immediately apparent until he came to a complete stop on the porch stoop.

Everett had powdered his arms.

He motioned in a languorous way for his men to come inside, and that was when I saw they had not known to wear slips. The light sailed through thin jersey, x-raying them one by one as they passed over the threshold, their voices dying, their flowered chests filling the house with color and sudden sculpture.

I couldn't eat.

My mother and father must have had one of their little conferences; they came into my room before they went to bed to see if I was still watching the party, which by now was full of smoke. The three of us sat awhile in the dark. I knew this sitting in the dark, together, was for me. They were trying to figure out how to tell me, how to help me sort out the mystery of a man's character. Dad cleared his throat and Mom said matter-of-factly that she didn't think much of Everett's little party. His bachelor celebration must have been what she was trying to tell me. Dad said it was badly timed. He wished there had been something we could have done for her. He'd finally learned she was staying with her sister. "She's a very smart woman," my father said, "by all reports."

I didn't appreciate them snooping on my feelings. What did *they* know?

"He might catch that man!" I said, suddenly angry, my hands under the sheets covering my breasts. Didn't they realize about the tissues? All anyone had to do over there was move a hair and those tissues would leap across the floor.

Well, Dad said, maybe so, maybe so, but he knew it was unfortunately timed; he didn't think Everett was fooling anybody much.

"But you don't know," I said, turning my face away from them. "You don't really know." My folks seemed like two yokel-dokels in their piped pajamas. Dad had to be up at five on Sundays, and in my imagination I made those light tissues leap up into the air while they dreamed. My innocent parents would be very surprised tomorrow if Everett caught that thief.

But when they left me alone finally, I couldn't get out of my mind the odd way the swinging pocketbooks had looked. They seemed misshapen to me or unclasped, and I closed my eyes to see them once more out there on the long arms of the boys, to see them lightly swinging until the big truth hit me over the head. All the pocketbooks were empty! Men like these didn't know to put anything inside, and a real thief would see this at a glance. He would see without coming near the house. They could pile a whole host of flat ladies' handbags up to Jesus if they wanted, but a real thief would be long gone by now. I thought of Everett's wife, in Miami. And how tomorrow all those boys — and the big chief as well — would sleep away the day over there like dead men, right through church and Sunday school.

DOCTOR
NORMAN VINCENT
PEALE

In 1955 my parents decided to go ahead and take Jeanie to the asthma clinic in Atlanta. We'd been moved to the Everglades, to a little church in Ochopee on the Tamiami Trail. Something in the new place had made my sister's condition worse — the milfoil, the hydrilla, some imported new weed, a hurricane letting down great pieces of sky. When a specialist suggested she go to an asthma clinic in Atlanta, Jeanie said she didn't mind as long as it was straight up in the air.

Since they couldn't take me with them, they had to find a place for me. Our great-aunt Dove in Valdez was the obvious person to leave me with for a month. My grandmother's new beliefs had left me shy of her, and my mother had observed how reluctant I was to talk to Grandma over the phone. Besides, Aunt Dove had gotten on the stick and sent me an invitation days before Mom had thought to make any other arrangements for me. She wrote as always on bond letterhead from the First Bank of Valdez, where my great-uncle Wesley had been president until he died. She said it was important for me to keep up my piano lessons and she had a Steinway, after all. No one played it now, she wrote. It sat there looking lonely, she added.

On all our visits, I'd seen the Steinway in her living room. Fat-legged and staunch, spiteful of women and children, the piano was kept polished by her maid, Annie — polished like the top of my late uncle's head.

"Have a ball," Jeanie said and laughed.

Whenever she rode in the car now, Jeanie reached for the little strap by her head and hung on as we went over bumps. I told her she was being pathetic on purpose. Mom had already started her on boiled rice and soybean milk, which we were all supposed to taste. Soybean was going to make us smell bad, I said, which caused an argument between me and Dad, and by the time they dropped me in Valdez I was glad to be rid of them.

After one week at Aunt Dove's mansion (it both was and wasn't), I was homesick. Aunt Dove didn't help matters one morning by telling me we had an appointment over at Wesley Bethel Methodist with a man from Southern Bell Telephone. "He wants to tell us about a demonstration he does for church groups," she said. I loved my aunt as much as anyone could have expected of me, but my loneliness that morning was a taste in my mouth. We were standing in the pantry off the kitchen, where she'd had me set up the ironing board. The scorched quilted cover was as old as my mother. Aunt Dove was teaching me how to do puffed sleeves.

"The man's name is Mr. Bishop," she said, touching the iron lightly to the fabric without making a crease. She lifted her blue head with the famous permanent waves forming peaks and valleys; they'd always reminded me of the psalm "I will lift up mine eyes unto the hills." I knew what a big shot my great-aunt was in Valdez. She was wearing a set of enameled combs a mission home had sent her from Korea. "Before we leave," she said, "you might want to freshen up." She held out the finished product. In the strong light the sleeve glowed from the inside, like a white blowfish.

Valdez, Florida, had one intersection, where a light flashed *caution* in all four directions. Just that afternoon, without my aunt's knowledge, Charlie Cope had put up a neon sign above the diner across from Uncle Wesley's bank.

"What kind of monkey business is that?" Aunt Dove said, pulling us over to the curb. Her gray Cadillac was eight years old, but I knew she'd never once hit a curb with it.

"It looks like celery," I said.

The neon celery stalk was not quite lit up yet. It sat above the skyline flickering weakly on one side; its new cool gases were as pale as sea water.

"I don't understand this," Aunt Dove said. She went in to talk to Mr. Cope about it, but by the time she came out, the stalk was brighter than her wildest dreams. The twenty-foot green tubes had filled out from the base; and now they tapered, realistically, in and out again before a spray of leaves rounded the whole thing off at the top.

When we got to the church parking lot, she stopped the

car with the hand brake. Some "irresponsible" party had propped open the door of Fellowship Hall with a cinder block. Aunt Dove said she'd have to speak to Lurleen, the cleaning woman, about it. And then as a final insult, the man from the phone company, her Mr. Bishop, turned out to look suspiciously like a salesman. She'd dressed up for a vice-president; this man was someone who took his hands out of his pockets a little too late to be really polite. His suit was as shiny as the cinnamon glaze on a cruller. When he bowed, he said he was delighted. I felt my aunt stiffen. She wouldn't shake his hand. He was shuffling around on linoleum that she paid to have buffed once a month with commercial equipment.

"I think we've made a mistake," she began. "When you called the other day about your demonstration . . ."

"Direct Dialing," Mr. Bishop said. He had burly temples dramatically whiter than the rest of his hair. He was straight and tan. Everything older about him looked premature. "We call it Direct Dialing."

"And *we* are a church," Aunt Dove explained. "I shouldn't have had you come all the way out here. I could have saved you the hot roads." My aunt looked at his shoes as though he might have walked all the way from Orlando.

"Mrs. Weston, Direct Dialing makes an educational demonstration for family groups. I'll set up a speaker so everyone can hear."

"We would never have need for a loudspeaker, Mr. Bishop."

"So they can all hear the call being dialed *direct*. If you have businessmen at your gathering, I'll let them call long-distance clients. We can call your service boys at Camp Lejeune. And your college boys."

"We only have one young person away at school right now," Aunt Dove said. "Her mother calls her in Winter Park every day, Mr. Bishop. It's a local call." My aunt's smile was unkind, but the man remained as innocent and untouched as any pro.

"Mrs. Weston, when I come out here with my equipment for a demonstration, I'll give out the code numbers you're all going to have real soon." Mr. Bishop had tricky hands. He began folding a large plaid handkerchief in squares until it disappeared. Vanished. "A child can direct-dial his grandmother in California!"

California. She was forced to be rude. "When, Mr. Bishop? That's my question. When would it ever be appropriate for you to come out here with your equipment?"

"At one of your potluck dinners, Mrs. Weston."

We didn't say potluck dinners in the South; we said covered-dish suppers. But the man was right on target and he knew it: congealed salads shaped like hearts, pineapple rings, upside-down cakes, and all those families sitting around the tables afterward, stirring Sanka. Family night. From the looks of him Mr. Bishop was the kind of man who could walk around and chat with the shy people. He could get an unmarried man to dial up his mother — the strong voice of a very old lady warbling over the speakers without benefit of an operator.

Mr. Bishop turned to the south wall, where they'd put up a Boy Scout flag and a half-dozen butterflies covered with wax paper. Farther on was a set of photographs commemorating the milestones of the church — award dinners and ground breakings. In the photographs the visiting clergymen looked like bowling pins.

"Do you people have a bishop?" Mr. Bishop suddenly asked out of nowhere. He did not seem to be making the least fun of the coincidence with his own name. "What if we put in a call to your bishop at the end of your demonstration? You could arrange ahead of time for him to be ready to say a closing word or maybe even a prayer." Mr. Bishop's voice had gone a little oily. My aunt was too shaken by his clairvoyance to notice it. That very morning she'd received a postcard from her bishop showing a cathedral formation of stalactites. He'd written her from Mammoth Cave.

"Do you know Bishop Branscomb?" she asked.

"No, ma'am, I've never had the pleasure. But you'd be able to direct-dial him. It would be a good way to end the evening. You have no idea how honored I'd be."

Lurleen put her head through the swinging doors from the kitchen and waved at Aunt Dove. "Warm, ain't it?"

Aunt Dove smiled, and by the time she looked again Mr. Bishop had folded his hands just under his chin. All his fingers were entwined except for the steeple. For the first time, he looked like an executive who'd been cruelly demoted to Sales and Demonstration in the last years of his long, faithful service to the phone company. I felt my aunt's shame as I stood beside her, looking at the individual half moons in the man's fingernails; they rose one by one on their separate horizons. She opened her mouth to speak; she had been so very rude.

"Mrs. Weston?" he interrupted. "With your permission, what if we were to telephone a long, long distance indeed?"

Aunt Dove stared at him. He was leaning toward her now as if he were going to ask her, pointblank, to make a trip with him to the Holy Land. "What if we were to call New York at the end of your demonstration? I have connections with a very important man up there."

Aunt Dove's hand moved involuntarily to her throat. "I hardly think that would be necessary."

We heard Lurleen banging around in the cupboards behind the swinging doors. She broke into song just as Mr. Bishop offered to end Aunt Dove's covered-dish supper with a call to Norman Vincent Peale. Had she ever heard of him, he asked her tenderly, the Reverend Doctor Norman Vincent Peale?

Florida's tremendous wealth is visible everywhere now. But back then it was only a few grand houses resting on a barely perceptible bit of high ground. Flat central Florida towns in the fifties all had a Hillside Street, a Hillcrest Street, or a Hillview Street, where the wealthy sat a little above sea level. As soon as you passed the last house — its portico held up by six white columns — you came to a railroad track with a spectacular junkyard on the other side.

Monday we were out in Aunt Dove's front yard on Hillcrest, cutting an armful of roses, when Mr. Bishop, his heart visible in his face, drove up in a beat-up Ford. When he got out he was holding a ceramic mug from the diner, the kind that is almost heavier empty than full. He was embarrassed he hadn't phoned to say he was coming over. "I was anxious to know if you'd heard from Doctor Peale," he called out bravely to us from the road. "I asked his office to contact you here."

Aunt Dove slowly removed her hat and garden gloves; she took my arm and ceremoniously walked me across the lawn toward him. She had a spring-fed lawn that felt like the carpeting in a luxury liner. Her birdbath was from Canada. "I haven't heard from anyone, Mr. Bishop."

Across the road Mr. Beasley's tractor, pulling a wagonload of garbage, came rushing toward us through a lot of white pine. Mr. Beasley had no business taking short cuts to the dump like that. When he made a sharp left into the road, he tipped his hat at Aunt Dove and calculated the turn badly. When it looked as if he wasn't going to be able to keep from nudging Mr. Bishop's Ford, he had to grind himself to a stop.

"Do you know whose car this is, Miss Dove?" Beasley yelled from high up on his tractor seat.

"For heaven's sake, Lonny," Aunt Dove said.

But Lonny Beasley went on. "Ma'am, they're going to have to *move*. I can't back this thing up without jackknifing." To prove it, Lonny began backing himself into an acute angle that drew the loaded wagon against the rear end of the Ford. Mr. Bishop said, "Hold it, hold it," but he didn't have time to shield himself properly from a packing crate easing in slow motion out of the wagon. We heard it crack him hard on the head before he slumped to the ground. Aunt Dove was powerless for a moment until Mr. Beasley asked if she thought he was dead.

"Oh, don't act foolish!" she shouted. She was already on her knees, her neat head pressed to Mr. Bishop's chest. "You get in that house and call Doctor Weems right now. Hurry up! Tell Annie to come out here." She'd put her hand to Mr. Bishop's forehead. I heard her say, "The poor man is losing his life's blood."

"It's all right, Mrs. Weston," Mr. Bishop murmured. "I have received a glancing blow."

. . .

Doctor Weems weighed well over three hundred pounds. He had little patience for being called to examine a man who appeared to have fainted on Uncle Wesley's old campaign bed. But by the time I was sent by Aunt Dove with a Coca-Cola, Doctor Weems had come to his own conclusions upon learning Mr. Bishop's account of the accident, and he didn't care if I heard: Aunt Dove deserved a *lawsuit*. She'd prevented the purchase of a real garbage truck in Valdez for two years. In fact, he said, yelling at Mr. Bishop, there were so many things she'd prevented in Valdez, it would do a whole lot of good if someone sued her to Hades and back.

Uncle Wesley's large paneled room was just off the downstairs hall, and I'd only been in that room once, when Uncle Wes had taken me in there himself to get some gift bonds out of his safe and had showed me rather proudly the humor slogan he'd made into a paperweight: OLD BANKERS NEVER DIE, THEY JUST LOSE INTEREST. Over that saying, he'd wheezed and wheezed.

Framed photographs of my uncle and his hunting friends in high-water boots hung on all the walls. Now, in the center of all this, the patient, Mr. Bishop, lay in smiling pain; he'd folded his hands over his chest while Doctor Weems stood beside him, repeating that he ought to sue. A phone began ringing somewhere deep in the house. "That might be the call from Norman Vincent Peale," Mr. Bishop said, and the doctor took this non sequitur so bitterly, I thought the exasperation would make him burst. He hauled himself around and yelled at me, "You go tell your aunt this man has had a concussion!"

·   ·   ·

Mrs. Weems paid us a call that afternoon, asking after Mr. Bishop. She stood at the front door holding a covered dish. She had brand-new bright blue potholders. The casserole was chicken, she said, straining to see beyond me into the house. Mrs. Weems was sorry to have heard about the accident. "Is he a relative?" she asked when she was finally seated.

"No, no," Aunt Dove said. She looked the doctor's wife over.

"My husband tells me your guest is expecting a telephone call from Norman Vincent Peale."

"Yes," Aunt Dove said. She looked at me this time.

"Isn't that amazing!" Mrs. Weems said.

"Yes," Aunt Dove said, so that finally Mrs. Weems simply had to get up and leave. I watched her sprightly retreat down the front walk. She was disappointed, but she strolled purposefully away from us, clutching her blue potholders.

I never heard Aunt Dove speak to anyone between Monday and Thursday while Mr. Bishop recuperated from his concussion and the Weemses spread their version of what happened around town. She refused to acknowledge to me or Annie that there was anything unusual in Mr. Bishop's staying with us. I knew I ought to say something in my weekly letter to my parents. I knew an adult would make casual mention of this to someone in the family. But there was no way I could manage casualness after my great-aunt handed out the stamp. She pressed it into my palm, closed my fist on it, lingered with a pause that, in some other context, might mean, "You're good to write your mother." But now it didn't mean that.

I was excited when I woke in the mornings now, even though we all moved around the house more serenely than ever to do our chores — a few hours every morning on the grounds, an hour helping Annie dust the wainscoting. The rest of the day we spent reading. We preferred biographies in the afternoon and fiction at night. Nothing here was anyone else's business. From time to time Aunt Dove would give me an appreciative look that went beyond my being a pleasure to have. It was a look of gratitude that it was I who was there and not some less feeling child.

Meanwhile, Mr. Bishop, lying quietly in Uncle Wesley's room, was presumed to sleep, though once when the door inched open, I thought I heard him humming. I thought I heard the desk chair squeak. And I thought I saw Mr. Bishop handling my uncle's leather artifacts.

Annie brought him his food on a tray. All he wanted was to be informed as soon as Norman Vincent Peale telephoned, and once he asked if there was a copy of Doctor Peale's famous book anywhere in the house. By midweek we felt sorry for him. He got up Wednesday morning and took breakfast at the table, but no one had called. No friend or relative; no colleague from the telephone company. "What a beautiful home you have, Mrs. Weston," he said, sighing, on his way back to bed.

Aunt Dove finally broke down after lunch on Thursday and called her minister.

Reverend Samuels had a pleased, silvery look about him. I knew immediately that he'd not heard a thing about Aunt Dove's predicament. A former district superintendent, way past retirement by now, Reverend Samuels was a temporary replacement for the regular pastor, who'd had a heart attack a while back on a trip to Fernandina.

Over coffee, Mr. Bishop told Reverend Samuels, man to man, about progress and the Communications Industry. "Most people find Direct Dialing a glimpse into the future."

"Oh, I guess so!" Reverend Samuels kept saying. "I guess so!" The old man would brighten like that for a moment ("I think I've heard about it"), but then he would fade and seem not to understand a thing. He was a dear man and not long for this world. As my grandmother would have said, he was already looking at the Bright Angel.

However, at one moment in the conversation Reverend Samuels recovered his old ministerial skill. He asked, "But how is Miss Dove going to choose which parishioners will place the calls?" His frown was earnest and practical all of a sudden. "She'll have to make them draw straws, I suppose."

My poor aunt had been about to offer him more coffee. "What do you mean?" she said.

"This Direct Dialing!" Reverend Samuels said. "They'll all want to try it."

"Of course they will!" Mr. Bishop boomed and went on to tell Reverend Samuels of the plan to dial Norman Vincent Peale.

"Now who is that?" the old man asked. Was it possible he'd never heard of him? We could never be sure, because all he ever said after that was "New *York!* How wonderful!" And it was the last thing he said when he was finally escorted to the door. "New York."

When Mr. Bishop and I were left alone for a moment, he

said he wanted to show me a trick he could do with his fork.

"You're feeling better, aren't you?' I said.

"Watch this," he said, plucking hard on the tines. When a single note rang out, I nodded at him.

"No, wait, that's not the trick! While it's vibrating you secretly touch the handle of the fork to the table. And you divert your audience's attention like this." Mr. Bishop was pointing his free hand here and there over the glasses. He was secretly pressing the ringing fork on the table to make it sing again and again, but it looked exactly the other way around — as if, on the downbeat of his free hand, the singing came from separate pieces of Aunt Dove's Fostoria. The tall goblets, like choirboys, gave him back sweet B-flats on cue.

Meanwhile, she stood at the door from the hall looking a little horrified.

"Miss Dove," he said, "what's the matter?"

"It's New York," she said, "on the telephone."

"Ah," Mr. Bishop said. We watched him get up from the table and fold his napkin slowly as if it were a surplice. Before he left the room, he paused. "The trick doesn't work at every table. You have to have real sterling. Real crystal."

Aunt Dove had only spoken to a secretary, but Mr. Bishop said he'd talked with Doctor Peale himself.

"He's agreed?" Aunt Dove asked.

Indeed he had! Doctor Peale had suggested July 15, Mr. Bishop announced. He handed Aunt Dove a small wallet calendar, which she took from him, stunned, as if she were drawing it from a pack of playing cards. Mr. Bishop spoke in the low, matter-of-fact voice of a good businessman. "We can dial him directly at his office at the Marble Collegiate Church. I told him *you* would be placing the call yourself."

"But the man is very famous," Aunt Dove said. She sat down at the table. "Did you tell him about the speakers? He didn't mind the loudspeakers?"

Mr. Bishop eased into the chair next to her on the long side of the table. "I usually use one speaker, Miss Dove." His eyes moved over her face. "If you think we need several, I'm sure I can get all you want."

"Oh, no, I only meant . . ." she said.

He was on his feet again. "My dear Miss Dove." He looked as though he was remembering how things used to be when he was a younger man with power. "I'll get you three or four speakers. I'll get you all the speakers I can put my hands on." And that afternoon he finally drove back to Orlando or wherever it was he lived.

Already Aunt Dove suspected he lived in his car.

In church the following Sunday, Reverend Samuels made an announcement about Aunt Dove's Direct Dialing demonstration. We began taking calls from people wanting to know how she was going to decide which loved one, which son or daughter or in-law would be dialed. Most people did not want to draw straws, we were told. Most people thought certain calls would not be as appropriate to make as others. The Davises would want their boy in Ohio to be dialed, for instance, but he'd never lived in Valdez. The Davises joined the church after John was married, if we recalled. The bride was from New Jersey. It wouldn't be as interesting to hear conversations with people the rest

of the congregation had never had the pleasure of knowing. There was Trudy, who hadn't seen her son in five
years and was proud of him now. But he'd never come to
church as a boy. Unfortunately, he'd driven around in that
car, if we recalled. Wouldn't it be nice if there was some
way to telephone people we could all enjoy about the
same? It was helpful to think of people who were naturally
good on the phone, who could tell interesting things about
how they were and what they were doing. It was a talent.
Professor Donaldson. Now there was a very entertaining
sort of person, although he hadn't left behind relatives
when he moved. Some wouldn't think it fair to call him
when there were so many we could call who were related
to someone. Mrs. Eldridge in Macon. She was both interesting and related. Of course, if we were going to call her,
we'd have to be sure to warn her first. It would only be
polite to give her a chance to think about what she might
want to say.

At my piano lesson, the church organist told me to tell
Miss Dove that the organist's own niece in North Carolina
had just won a scholarship to Mercer College, and if her
niece wasn't a good candidate for a demonstration call, the
organist didn't know who was.

I walked back through town and saw Mr. Bishop's Ford
parked out in front of the diner. One of his taillights was
knocked out. A piece of the red glass jutted out at a ragged
angle, and when I reached out the piece came off in my
hand. I was planning to go in and sit with him if he saw me
from one of the diner windows, but someone coming out
of the hardware store waved to me instead. It was the
woman at the bank who loaded and unloaded the capsule
in the pneumatic tube.

"They say he's your aunt's *friend*," she called. She looked carefully in both directions before crossing the road. She was carrying her new broom.

"He's from the phone company," I said.

The woman gave his Ford a knowing look. "Yes," she said, "that's what we heard."

Aunt Dove and I were reading in the living room when Mr. Bishop showed up one evening in the middle of a thunderstorm, wearing no raincoat. He presented us with three cut gardenias. From his sister's place, he said.

Aunt Dove took him into the kitchen and had him take off his suit coat. He'd gotten soaked, running up the long walkway in the rain. Water beads stood up like sequins in his hair. It was the first time I knew Mr. Bishop smoked cigarettes. The dampness brought it out.

"You have a sister, Mr. Bishop?" Aunt Dove found a wooden hanger and put his coat in the pantry.

"Miss Dove, I never realized what a beautiful kitchen you have. It's prettier than any I've ever seen."

"Is that so?" Aunt Dove said.

"I came by to give you this book." Mr. Bishop had brought her *The Power of Positive Thinking*. When she stepped to take it from him, he seemed, lovingly, to withhold the book at the same time he offered it. "It's a present," he said. "It's been translated into seven languages."

"Well," she said and ran her hand over the cover. "This is kind of you." The brand-new copy snapped with a loud jazzy upbeat when she opened it. She studied an inscription he'd written on the flyleaf.

Mr. Bishop smiled at me.

Neither of them ever meant to use me, but, for the rest

of the courtship, one or the other would often turn around like that and I'd be standing there. "I'm not someone she's used to doing business with," he said, smiling. "She's sure put her trust in a low man on the totem pole, hasn't she?"

Aunt Dove's kettle suddenly made us all jump. She turned to a place in the wall where she kept the tea behind a set of miniature doors. Mr. Bishop said he thought it was clever to paper the doors into the wall like that so they were invisible.

"She could have her jewels hidden in there, for example."

For the next week, Mr. Bishop rang her almost every day from Cope's Diner and I was always running for the phone.

At Cope's they kept a telephone down below with the clean glasses. The waitress there would heave it up over the taps and put it down on the narrow serving counter. ("Help yourself.") I loved the spoons, the sifted clinks in the background, whenever he called. "This is the Bishop," he would say. "Tell her it's the Bishop on the line." I used to imagine him smoking and watching himself in the panel of mirrors. Behind him, the blue-suited men, having their afternoon coffee at Cope's, sat in vinyl booths that had been passed down several generations like church pews. They would have told their wives about seeing him at the counter every day. They'd have mentioned it across the road. At Aunt Dove's bank.

I remember him arriving at the house in sport shirts sometimes. Or perhaps it was only the one time, when he came saying he wanted to help her in the yard.

"If you like," she said, smiling when he took the snub-nose clippers in his hand and worked them expertly in the air. He bent over Aunt Dove's roses in a limber, familiar way, though he handled every stem and blossom as if it were handblown glassware. He winced when he snipped at the delicate stems.

He said in his opinion the state of Florida was the whole history of pruning and nothing less. He raised himself up and looked off into the next county. Few people realized this, he said. Every inch had had to be drained and tended. And now it was sure paying off. There was a farmer over in Zellwood who was shipping his celery to Finland, if we could imagine that. He bent down again and tried to look as if he knew what he was doing. Finland, he said. He'd been there once.

"My goodness," Aunt Dove said.

Oh, he had a real belief in travel. Last year he'd put twenty thousand miles on his car. Most of it right around here, he said, pointing to the ground.

I used to wander out to the road and sit in that car. His car excited me to the point of making my hands ache. Right away I found a loose garter clip in the glove compartment. It dangled by its hardware in two pink pieces, which I locked in place and put in my pocket. I found Aunt Dove's Reader's Digest Abridged Version of *The Mighty in a Storm* out there in his car. He had marked his place with a toothpick, mint-sealed in its own envelope. He had taken one of Uncle Wesley's advertising pens. County maps and real estate brochures lay around on the front seat, fading in the sun. A navy blue tie; a lipstick melting over and over again. On the back of a place mat from Cope's Diner, Mr. Bishop had sketched, with the precision of a draftsman, the neon celery stalk, cooling its heart in town.

· · ·

At Mr. Bishop's insistence, we began calling my parents long distance in Atlanta. We were Direct Dialing pioneers; the calls were free with the code numbers he gave us. He and my aunt would go off to the kitchen and leave me to say whatever I wished.

Hearing my folks' voice was thrilling, since the more I spoke with them, the more distant they became in light of this new and subtle sort of lying I did. At least it was new to me.

"Are you having a good time?" my mother would ask, apologetic that I'd had to be farmed out for so long. This had never happened in our mild history of upheavals.

"I'm having the best time of all," I told her. That was the truth, but there were some omissions in it. I used to hang up the phone, my very bowels slightly loosened at the fear and pleasure of my mother's never having the least notion what was transpiring.

I'd rejoin Aunt Dove and Mr. Bishop in the kitchen, where Mr. Bishop might be carrying on, casually: "Someday an asthmatic like your sister will be able to dial up people from the middle of a desert on a cordless telephone. And you'll have one in your car."

But in the meantime, he said, there was no reason why people shouldn't have more telephones, period. For a while it seemed that he installed a new extension in the house every day, until Aunt Dove finally made him stop. She didn't want one in her *bedroom,* she said, laughing, and besides, you could hear us ringing all the way out in the road.

"Good!" Mr. Bishop said. "Good!"

A week before the Direct Dialing demonstration, a sharp, color-coordinated woman came to the house in the late morning. Tall, high-chested, she was one of the women from the church, dressed to visit. She said if I'd take her to the sun porch, please, she'd wait there while I went outside to announce her. Through the glass jalousies we could see Aunt Dove standing with Mr. Bishop by the oleander behind the house. Her hat strings were tied around her waist. The hat hung carelessly, like a satchel, low on one hip.

"Is that Reverend Samuels out there with her?" the visitor asked, putting her hand on my arm. She said it was convenient to find the two people she needed to see that afternoon in one place. She drew her purse into a hollow under that high chest of hers. She was preparing to follow me out.

"That's Mr. Bishop," I told her, feeling the cords in my neck go as taut as a clothesline. The woman's head was already craning forward. There was the telephone man pointing out something in the oleander, and it was shocking, even for me, to see how Aunt Dove refused to turn and follow his hand. She was staring at his profile. When a burst of sunlight turned the two of them almost white, we saw their shoulders touch. It was as if the intense, buzzing sun had dissolved their insubstantial lines into heat waves and simply swayed them, inevitably, together.

"Mercy," the woman said. She handed me her calling card, which, to put it one way, I swallowed as soon as she left. I trudged up to my room and sat for an hour, reliving every blunder. Helpless, I'd followed as the woman returned to the front hall and slowly adjusted her hat at the mirror. She was *sorry* to have come at such an inconvenient time, she said, studying herself closely, her nose an inch from the foxed glass. She asked me if she was to assume that was *his* car then. Out there in the road.

Aunt Dove may have forced someone to tell her. She may have forced it gently at the bank when she asked some officer in passing if he and his wife were planning to hear Norman Vincent Peale on Wednesday night. She may have put a patient, encouraging hand on his desk and waited sympathetically until he finally confided in her: some people were saying she'd arranged this supper to accommodate her friend. Some of them worried that old Reverend Samuels had been a little misled.

Mr. Bishop had no reliable sources. And no way to really prepare himself. When Aunt Dove expressed a few doubts on Monday in order to help him get ready for at least a mild upset of his plans, he rolled back on his heels. He'd invented positive thinking, in case she didn't know. She'd best get busy and read the book.

He'd bought himself a blue suit that afternoon. Because of his height he had to tilt Uncle Wesley's free-standing mirror twice to see all of himself in it. He told us Reverend Samuels had stopped him on the street to ask if he needed help with any last details. How wonderful it all was, Reverend Samuels had said. He was expecting the largest crowd since the pageant. Forty families might turn out for an evening like this.

I felt my aunt reach out and steady herself. She put her arm around my shoulders. "Frank, you look very nice in that suit." And that night I took a call from Frank after my aunt had gone to bed with a sick headache.

"It's the Bishop," he whispered, his voice low in his

happiness. "Tell her he called to check on her, to see if she was sober or not."

In the morning I found Aunt Dove seated across from Annie, polishing. "He called last night," I said. I was confused by now. I was in this thing deep, but ignorant and torn, and always thrilled. "You were asleep."

"Dreaming," she said. She smiled at Annie, not meaning to exclude me. "I suppose I was dreaming."

But later that morning we were all bounced back to rightness and health. Mr. Bishop took us for a long drive in the Cadillac. We were taking Annie to Zellwood to see her new grandbaby. Things fit together again — him behind the wheel, all of us beaming; me, the child they would have had. I knew they felt it too. The sex was palpable in the car. I sentimentalized it into the very shape of my self, remembering how, not three weeks ago, she'd tried to entertain me rather stupidly by sitting me down in front of a pink suit box filled with makings for Christmas ornaments. I was supposed to use my imagination while she served someone out on the sun porch. Iced coffee on lacquered trays. I'd thrown my head in my arms.

Now I sat thinking about the complicated beads making up a person's life — how one's hair is not always gray, how one is not so much a fixed body as a set of poses put together in a child's flipbook: begin at the beginning and all the scenes of my aunt's life moved as one; the young and old in her joined at the head as I watched jumping girleens of all ages, all the same woman.

Annie's daughter and her husband lived in a house built on the edge of twenty acres of celery.

But everything in Florida is cut by July. The fields looked as dark as pitch. This must be the best muck soil in the whole country, Mr. Bishop bragged to the husband.

"Except in California," the husband said.

Well, Mr. Bishop said, he'd seen firsthand that they didn't have anything out there we couldn't get better.

"Except they grows rice out there and artichokes too."

And who eats *them*, Mr. Bishop wanted to know.

"Not me," the husband said, laughing.

Aunt Dove came out with lemonade. The three of us sat alone on the edge of the porch while they visited inside. The baby was only a week old and cried with no emotion. My aunt dangled her feet off the porch. A moment or two later Mr. Bishop raised his glass and rested it on top of my head. "Your aunt's brave," he said. He removed the glass and kissed the wet spot in my hair. "Or else she doesn't see I'm a completely unsuccessful person."

"But you're not. That's not true," she said, embarrassed.

"Of course it's true!" He poked me in the ribs. "It's true, isn't it?" Then he put his arm around me and squeezed me sideways. "I'll have to look at the bright side and hope for the best. Since she's so brave."

The night of the covered-dish supper, Mr. Bishop had not envisioned an empty parking lot. He pulled his Ford up among the two cars and three old pickup trucks sitting alone at odd angles. Fellowship Hall looked as if it had been lit up on the wrong night. I'd gone out to the lot to wait for him.

"Are you coming in?" I called.

He turned off his engine and drummed his fingers on the

dashboard while he finished his cigarette. He finally yelled back. "What in the world happened? Where are all these families he was talking about?"

"I don't know," I said. "There're a few."

Inside, Reverend Samuels and his wife stood with my aunt Dove and three farm families who'd driven in from Kissimmee and Chuluota. One prominent Valdez couple was there — the Thomases. They were retired missionaries from China who showed their slides once a year. And Lurleen was there. ("It's cooled up some, ain't it?") She'd been hired to wash dishes.

"Well, well," Mr. Bishop called out. He paused and rocked on his feet. "Well, what do you know."

"Good evening," someone called. "Come on in."

The farmers were hungry and wanted to get the show on the road. "Come on in." There were only four or five casseroles on one table. The casserole lids, dripping on their undersides, had already been removed to the kitchen. The tinfoil seals were broken and everything smelled like cheese. We filed by, afraid to dish up too much. No one had a thing to say.

While we ate, Mr. Bishop sat at one end of another long table with one of the farmers' wives, who nursed a baby on a bottle. He talked to the wife to keep from having to look at my aunt. For a while he was giddy and in a loud voice offered to feed the baby, though the young woman waved him off, laughing. She had no idea who he was and asked him politely where he was from.

During dessert, he set up his equipment. By then I could see he was deeply hurt. It came out as bravura. After he connected a long extension line from the church office telephone, he made a great show of setting up six loudspeak-

DOCTOR NORMAN VINCENT PEALE

ers. He hauled them in one by one and pushed Aunt Dove's feelings to the brink. She had to get up from her chair and go open a window wider to keep from showing her emotion. By now he was making loud exclamations into the empty expanse of Fellowship Hall. The wives all thought he was a card.

"If I'd brought one more speaker, you each could have had one," he told the farmers' boys, who covered their mouths to keep from giggling. One of the lanky older boys asked how many of those gall dern things did he have anyway?

"More than *you'll* ever see," Mr. Bishop said. His face was flushed. Finally he shrugged and looked at Aunt Dove, whose eyes were bright and misty. He had to turn away again in order to go on and lead the faithful troops. "Which of you wants to make the first call?" he said. He sighed and looked at his watch. "We have until eight."

One of the farmers asked if he could call a sister of his in Pensacola.

His wife said, "She'll be surprised, won't she, Ned?"

"Candid Camera!" Ned said.

I cowered in my seat at the other end of the table, watching him write out the secret numbers. "Just dial those first." He spoke to them kindly now. He sat back in his chair while the calls went through and gazed at the dried butterflies on the wall. Reverend Samuels's wife leaned over and asked *sotto voce* about his accident.

"We understand you were indisposed," she said. She was younger and more engaging than her husband. "Have you been in the area many years, Mr. Bishop?"

He stared at her. "A few."

"We're all so curious how you got to know our Dove Weston? She's a favorite, you know." Reverend Samuels's wife was enormously sympathetic. "Everyone loves her," she explained.

"I can see that," Mr. Bishop said.

Norman Vincent Peale made history on July 15, 1955, when my great-aunt Dove dialed him at his office at Marble Collegiate. The famous minister spoke to us as a friend would have. He had educated himself about Valdez, he said. He had looked us up on the map, and one of his business friends had informed him we were near Sanford, the Celery Capital of the World.

His short talk was about capitals of the world and how you find them wherever people worked courageously together for common goals. But he'd designed his meditation to sound like a real phone conversation, and he'd interrupt himself to let my aunt reply and say things back to him. "Well, it's very kind of you," she would say; "you are very kind to say so." She held the receiver tentatively, the feedback of her own voice through all those speakers making her shy. Finally Doctor Peale rang off graciously. He said if Aunt Dove ever came to New York she could dial him direct there, too. She should be *sure* to call him.

She said she hoped he'd do the same if he ever traveled to Florida.

He would! He would indeed.

"Good-bye," she said.

Good-bye! He wished us all happy, productive lives.

Aunt Dove put down the receiver. There was a moment of silence in which none in the gathering moved until Mrs.

Samuels got up with great ceremony to kiss Aunt Dove on the cheek.

Someone took her cue and led us in a round of applause, which Mr. Bishop suddenly accepted himself by making a deep, jerky bow that accidentally collapsed a wooden chair behind him. The noise caused the minister's wife to step back. Then the applause faltered when we all began to hear that he was making a loving farewell to Aunt Dove. He used rather high-flown sentences: that she would live in his heart forever and something about begging her leave. Someone standing behind him chuckled in confusion; it was only that it was all so courtly. Then Mr. Bishop turned on us. The faithful. Did we value what we had here in Mrs. Weston? he demanded. Perhaps we did, but he seriously doubted it. What did we really know about her? He glared at us. "*She* knows about courage," he said, "although I certainly won't require any more of her courage from now on. And I hope you'll tell the others. They can all be assured. Will you tell them for me?"

No one moved.

"Well?" he said. "Yes or no?"

Reverend Samuels was summoned back into the world of mortal affairs. We watched the shaken minister stop a few feet from Mr. Bishop and speak to him as one would speak to a man about to leap from a building. "My dear sir, come with me," he said and led Mr. Bishop quietly from the hall.

Aunt Dove had planned months before to have Mrs. Padilla, a Cuban seamstress, come stay with her in July for the reupholstery work in the living room. They set up in front of the large windows, at which Aunt Dove would stand and gaze out while she waited for him to call. Her Black Prince roses were all gone now, and she neither confided in nor hid a thing from me. Whenever I came within a few feet of her, she would meet me the rest of the way. She would take up my hand.

``He'll call,'' she'd say. ``He has to recover.'' Her lips had grown so pale. ``I don't want you worrying.''

In a week she tried telephoning him herself. An operator in Orlando told her there was no number listed in his name. Aunt Dove dialed all the other Bishops in the area, but none of them turned out to be a sister. Annie finally told her to ask for him at work.

``I might embarrass him,'' Aunt Dove said.

``Pooh,'' Annie said, and, when a secretary in Personnel told Aunt Dove they had no record of his employment with Southern Bell, Aunt Dove snapped, ``Don't be ridiculous,'' and hung up on the woman.

People stopped by to call on her again, but she sent me or Annie to the door with a jar of guava jelly. I developed ramrod composure, and everyone must have thought me very ugly.

After two more weeks we took the Cadillac to Orlando to do some shopping, and on the way out of town she kept her eye on the stalk and shot right through to the other side.

She made a stop at the telephone offices in Orlando. While we waited outside in the dark car, Annie rested her head on the back of the seat and said, ``Lord God.''

It was the end of the month and I'd packed my bags to go home when the telephone finally rang the way it did whenever he called. The house clanged with bells, and I ran for the extension upstairs, overjoyed to hear him booming, "This is Norman Vincent Peale! I'd like to speak with Mrs. Weston."

I can remember storming through the house, looking for her. Something had been sitting, waiting for this moment when I could cavort and shout, "Aunt Dove, Aunt Dove, he's on the telephone!"

She looked up from her book.

"He's pretending to be Doctor Peale," I said. "Hurry."

She finally smiled at me, but she would not let me hug her.

I followed her to the old phone in the hall and watched her prepare herself. Without giving him a chance to say anything, she told him firmly that he must have received another glancing blow. "It's the only explanation for why you've been so rude." She was smiling in relief now. "Oh, Frank, I'm so glad." She wiped her cheek with the sleeve of her linen blouse. "I'm so glad, dearest."

She would have gone on had something not stopped her suddenly; she just listened, her eyes darting, as the real Doctor Peale told her politely that there must be some misunderstanding. It was he, Norman Vincent Peale, whom she might remember? They had spoken long distance several weeks ago? Did she remember? He had come to Florida after all, on a business trip. He was calling from Orlando to give his regards.

I watched her struggle to keep from breaking down — to keep from upsetting terribly the famous man.

"This is so kind of you," she managed to say. "Forgive me, I hardly expected this."

Ah well, it was his pleasure, his pleasure!

.   .   .

A few years later Direct Dialing became a reality. Everyone thought it was a great technological advancement, although once in a while we'd hear of people cheating the phone company outrageously until the system was perfected. A newspaper account told of a clever high school boy who could throw the coded tones over the wire with his own voice. He was calling strangers halfway around the world before he was caught.

My aunt Dove never had to read about that kind of monkey business. By then she'd passed away, and in the time between that summer and her death two years later, I was too far removed to keep the sweet edge on such a secret as that. Eventually, not long after I'd forgotten the nuances, I told my parents everything.

By the afternoon they'd showed up to take me home again, Aunt Dove and I were growing distanced, not knowing how, in front of others, to say good-bye. We'd have given ourselves away. I believe she put a stiff hand on my head and said I must write, and that moments later, in the car, my family assumed I'd been rescued.

"You've been so patient," my mother said. "I'm so proud of you."

After her funeral, someone found a little treasure my aunt Dove had sealed inside an almost blank envelope. I stared at my name written out in faint pencil strokes — so genteel, so like a great-aunt; my name looked as if it were already fading in and out from her effort to transmit a message to me from the other side of the grave. Before I could get the thing open, my hands were aching.

It was a letter from Doctor Peale, thanking her for her kind note of explanation. She need not have written any apology, he said. These little mix-ups were so frequent in life, and her moment of confusing him with someone else so forgivable. He recalled that when the arrangements were made, he'd not actually had the pleasure of speaking directly with her Mr. Bishop. In that she was mistaken. But, from everything she said, he sounded like a resourceful, wonderful, good-natured man whom he would like to meet someday. In the meantime, he hoped it wouldn't be inappropriate to send kind regards to them both? While he remained truly hers, NVP.

O FOR A
THOUSAND TONGUES
TO SING

WE HAD TO MOVE right out of the Everglades because of Jeanie; and at our new church in Pompano they
had a teenage boy named Lorin Grant, who, we were told,
wasn't quite right.

He got ideas.

Once, he'd climbed into a high-voltage area, and later
he'd been taken out of school because his only topic of conversation was disease. Most recently, however, he'd gotten
it into his head that his own next-door neighbors were test-
ing his honesty by leaving a silver dollar out on their side-
board for him to steal. He'd have seen it lying, innocent,
on a yellowed linen runner for his whole growing-up.
That's what people *meant*. And at a bright green party,
with them all outside visiting, their hot feet cooling in the
sprinkler, he'd gone in their house with a hammer, finally,
and put a penny nail as big as your finger through the silver
dollar and then on down into lovely, lovely wood.

· · ·

I daydreamed about Lorin Grant during school hours quite a lot on Fridays, because the Grants began having us over Friday nights. They told us that Jeanie and I would be important for Lorin to *be* with. But I thought the Grants were very unrealistic people. They were putting their heads in the sand. Jeanie and I weren't old enough to be Lorin's equals and I didn't think we did him any good. Around us he only acted like a robot; nothing more serious. He'd take our coats and do cadet pivots over to the coat closet with them. He pretended they'd trained him to say "Excuse me, please, I enjoyed my dinner" so he could rise from the table as if pulled up by his hair. He'd try to disappear through a crack in the door to his bedroom so we wouldn't see the empty fish tanks he kept back there for his hobby.

Leeches.

In the way people ordered tropical fish from specialized catalogues, Lorin Grant ordered leeches. They came through the mail. His parents told Jeanie and me about them so we wouldn't be alarmed if we ever saw them. They arrived sometimes all the way from Australia, packed in a little saline solution.

"They're interesting," Mrs. Grant claimed. "And not very big. If you saw that movie," she said, "they aren't like *those*."

"Small as the tip end of your finger," Mr. Grant said.

Mr. Grant was a sweet, pink-faced man with other grown children and a speedboat. He took us to a nearby lake to teach us to water-ski once. We were really dreadful on skis, and Lorin smirked the whole day from under a sun visor. But on another occasion Lorin had done something so humorous, my mother thought there was great reason to hope. She and Mrs. Grant and Lorin were in Green Haven's together when Mom told the man at the counter she wanted some of his preserves to take to a sick grandmother. "Mrs. Willis, I sure hope the wolf doesn't get us," Lorin had said. For a year my mother couldn't stop repeating the story on herself. She'd had on her short red cape — only lacking the hood — and there she'd stood at the counter, gesturing, middle-aged, telling about a sick grandmother.

If it made Lorin a genius (my mother was convinced it might), I couldn't see it; he'd have to prove it. And I was thinking all this out on a Friday morning in school, trying to imagine how it would be if he ever went berserk, how if I was lucky he might act up or roll around with one shoe off, when I suddenly felt my teacher's hand on my neck.

"You've dreamed away the whole morning," he said. "I hope you enjoy lunch better than you do me."

My teacher, Mr. Camfort, was the only World War II conscientious objector in Florida as far as anyone knew. He had continued to pay for his point of view by living in Pompano Beach with a very low social standing and almost no salary; he practiced celibacy and was talked about as being perfectly nice to anyone who was not a known fool. He didn't seem to mind his isolation. It was not difficult to see that his dapper exterior barely hid a fervent soul and that was why there was an ironic tone in all his judgments. Children learned quickly that his mind was never still; parents looked forward to running into him on the street. And now, with his hand on my neck, he was raising the old question: Why waste our time like this when we'd drawn the best teacher in the school? This was talk that excited us. We loved all instances of irony because it both made us think we were cuter than we were and hinted of bigger things in the world to come.

The atmosphere at lunch on that extraordinary Friday was the same as always: all over the cafeteria, under the globe lights, hung on long chains, the younger grades were seated and preparing to sing their class blessing — "Be present at our table, Lord" and the like. A group would end ". . . and grant that we / May feast in paradise with Thee" just as another started up on "Let no wars . . ." The latter, Mr. Camfort's own pacifist invention, was a favorite song of ours; at the end, our voices had to maneuver inside a strange minor key — ghostly and adult:

> Let no wars impede our thanking
> God above for this our bread
> That our song may *end* the battles,
> Let us feed on that instead. Amen.

The cafeteria acoustics were good, but the system of every class taking a turn was a nuisance. Those being served had to stop their assembly line of trays every few moments and wait. The serving ladies, worn out from the ritual, would dramatically arrest their great spoons in the air and look to heaven. All this stopping and starting.

We loved it. Once on the floor, we would try to get caught by the singing again so that we could freeze into statues — Red Light–Green Light — our steaming plates and milk bottles stopped dead in their tracks. The rule was that as long as we didn't move during an entire blessing, we could glance around and note the exaggerated poses of our friends and enemies, their arms gone rigid, their trays held up like burnt offerings.

And that was what I was doing in the middle of the cafeteria when I felt a safety pin come open and two halves of elastic fall away. In one second, my warm panties had landed on the tops of my shoes and shackled me at the ankles. Before I could look, I felt them, like candle tallow, growing cold. All their insides showed — all the hard nubs from one million turns in my mother's new automatic washer. For a moment I was sure I would faint. The first-grade class at Table 9 continued in languorous phrases — our smallest angels, fiercely *a cappella* and tender. And floating toward me, as if trying to rush to my aid through quicksand, Mr. Camfort in slow motion, the high voices approaching that highest minor shift, when the soul heaves to such a gorgeous suspiration of children singing, one feels oneself prepared, quite happily, to die.

I looked at him and bit back tears.

"Oh now, shush!" he said, taking my tray and shielding me from view as I did the terrible work of bending down and hiking up. I held the broken elastic under my dress and walked with him to Table 12. People said he had seized that prized place for his group long ago. From the beginning of my fortunate tenure with him, Table 12 had reminded me of the chosen people, the beloved disciples.

Mr. Camfort put down my tray and then examined the safety pin I'd used that morning. No, it was no longer serviceable, he said. On my way to the Girls I must pass by our room and open the center drawer of his desk. I would find another, larger pin in a cup on the left-hand side.

He nodded me away. I was excused.

·   ·   ·

The desk drawer was badly warped, but when it finally slid open, I looked and was immediately a candidate for reform. I drew back at my teacher's readiness.

Not just one but a whole hoop of brand-new safety pins — a whole continuum of bright silver and gold disasters — hung by their tails. I fingered them one by one, blaming my mother for the way ours at home collected in bottoms of sewing boxes and had to be torn away from old thread that had grown on them like plant tendrils. Mostly they were not to be found, and I hated the slamming scenes in which she threw open drawers, looking for the one she'd seen the day before but could not for the life of her remember where.

Dad might accidentally clear his throat or touch his tie clip.

"Oh, I'm coming!" she would mutter, her feelings hurt. She'd rake a straight pin from the windowsill above the sink and in the car tell me to be still and suck in while she wove the thing into the side seam of my dress. Like me, my mother cried more easily now. She took Dad's silences as reprimands — that she was untidy, maybe thoughtless. We all knew it was worse than that — that my father was, rather, on the moon. His mind took leisurely rambles into craters and valleys we never got to visit. Where did he get the time! His temperament gave him so much *more* of it than ours gave us. When my mother cried, we knew it meant that if we'd all been so what-is-a-man-profited, we'd have long gone to sea in a sieve.

"I'm pointing it up, honey," Mom would whisper to me. "I don't think it will stick you if I'm careful."

One of the teachers from a very high grade, from another building altogether, was happening by when she saw me, just then, about to take something from another teacher's desk, and hurried to the rescue of Mr. Camfort's things. Her shoes pounded the wooden floor. I was on the verge of suffering from a false accusation and got myself ready to heap coals of fire on her head when she realized what a terrible mistake she'd made.

"Oh, hello," she said, recognizing me right away and giving me no credit for anything criminal. "What's the matter?"

"My pants fell down in the cafeteria," I said. I was still holding them up under my dress. There'd been no venting of my public shame until now; it had taken a warm and sympathetic look to get my pride flowing. "Everyone saw," I said. "I'm not going back in there."

"Well, you don't have to," she said and sat down in Mr. Camfort's chair to hear details. Moments before, the shadow of my real advocate had been there to protect me. Now, I was ready to trade him in without a second thought.

"Do you know the same thing happened to me once in college?" the young woman said. "I was in a huge crowd of people, and there was nothing for me to do but step out of them and keep walking."

"Is that what you did?" I asked, quickening at this readiness beyond readiness — the deception it would have taken to pretend my own panties had not even belonged to me.

She said it was hardly her worst moment, and my heart raced to keep up with her. One time she had been in a women's rest room at the movies, she said. She assumed it was her sister in the stall next to her. She recognized her sister's handbag sitting on the floor, and when she reached under the partition for it, a total stranger had cried out, "Help, thief!"

But suddenly the woman was hugging me and going out the door. "I've got to run. You'll be fine. Just hold your head up for the rest of the afternoon." And I sat alone at Mr. Camfort's desk, feeling her physical presence leave me by degrees.

In a daze I went into the rest room and while there was struck by the thought of her stepping briskly over her shame and walking on. I was so inspired, I yanked and pulled at my pants until I'd gotten them over my oxfords. I wrapped them in a paper towel and buried them in the bottom of the wastebasket.

At first I was sure everyone on the playground would stop what they were doing. But most of them were running around, screaming. About what exactly? I could no longer remember. Imbeciles. I stood panning the scene — a killer's point of view. Old Mr. Camfort was in his usual shady spot, leaning against the building. He was taking his nap. He'd crisscrossed his arms above his belt with the bone buckle and closed his eyes. Half of us had not believed him when he'd told us that both he and President Eisenhower could actually fall asleep this way.

Each of my friends was shaking her head off; each looked as if she were being thumped like a dust mop. And the girls not feeling well swayed in sultry poses under the eaves. They were reading each other's lifelines. Without my panties on, to me the unfamiliar ground — flat and waxed like clay tiles — seemed twenty feet down.

That night at the Grants' house my heart banged in its cage, because I was home free for the one day, a teenager with the sheer gumption nobody had suggested was possible for me any time I wanted it. That night at the Grants' I just opened the door to Lorin's room to smoke the lonely boy out.

Lorin Grant looked up from what he was doing.

"I need a safety pin," I told him. "I have a rip in my dress."

He was writing at his desk. His hands were blue. Blue ink from his fountain pen had leaked while he'd been hard writing. I was interrupting honest effort. Paper lay thin and unlined, signaling his concentration. I knew whatever he was putting down was what separated him from the likes of someone like me, who, to date, had done no work that was not assigned by a teacher. That afternoon Mr. Camfort himself, writing our weekend homework on the blackboard, had hinted: someday, we would feel the motion of our thought beating as softly as the wings of a bat.

"What do you want?" Lorin asked, opening the long drawer of his desk, handing me a large safety pin.

My gaze must have flicked around his room. "Why aren't there fish in these tanks anymore?"

"There were never fish in them. Which one put you up to this? My mother or my father? I bet it was my father."

Red Light–Green Light. Memory arranging scenes conveniently into eerie still lifes. Lorin, pointing with his long weary hand to his hobby. The ostensible world. "Over there," he said. I was to have a look, if that's what I wanted, and then get out of his room.

The wall of fish tanks had seemed empty because the leeches were, indeed, very small. I had to go right up to the glass. I didn't understand the layout of things at first, although I identified the creatures right away; they were no bigger than small blisters and didn't move, which was not surprising. But they were attached, in each tank, to a rubber glove whose fingers pointed down, several leeches on each full finger.

"What are they doing?" I asked.

"Feeding," he said. The gloves were engorged. He had an arrangement with the local butcher, he explained, opening one of the wrists to show how the blood was poured in from there. Simple. This was his own original idea. And when I finally understood, I discovered I'd tucked each of my own hands into opposite armpits and was pressing down so hard I was cutting off my circulation.

Minutes later I followed Lorin out of his room, dazed, not wanting this to happen. He was walking straight for the door of the dining room to find out who was responsible for sending me. I could feel the heat coming out of his skin and the sweetish smell of the bewilderment and the humiliation he felt at being about to make a scene. The old curse of being Lorin seemed to have refallen on the house without anyone's knowing he was at that moment stalking the dark hall to sink the axe of his confusion into someone else's brain.

My parents hadn't any idea what it meant that he'd brought one of the fresh gloves with him to the table. He held it up to show his father what he should prepare himself for.

"What are you doing with that, son?" I remember Mr. Grant asking, getting up slowly, trying not to anger the boy further.

"I'm being sociable," Lorin said. His voice failed him. "I thought everyone might want to see this."

"Lorin," his mother said.

Mr. Grant began talking to his son in a monotone, and we could sense there was a chance Lorin would merely turn around and retreat. I saw then that whatever he suffered was as bad as razors moved backward across the soles of your feet. The boy walked on coal. He might turn away in a moment, or else begin to pull back his arm to throw the feeding contraption at his father or one of us. My parents seemed not to sense the worst, though I saw my mother bracing herself while Lorin moved his gaze from person to person until he finally settled on the centerpiece, a few white and red camellias, floating. Everyone studied the camellias, not wanting to watch how his brave eyes stared and then, hugely, filled with tears. He had such brimming, crystal waters in him. The two bright, hanging pools could fill teaspoons. His affliction seemed that he was not able to blink. That the world hung before him, brimming and magnified, swimming with light and diamonds and with no release.

"Help me, Noel," Mr. Grant said to Dad.

The men got on either side of him and took an arm and steered him back to his room, where they stayed until the demon had been more or less called out of him. Dad said they looked at his collection of medical books for a while and waited for him to find his voice, which he finally did, to talk about the way leeches were being used by science. Researchers, he explained to my father, were learning how to make anticoagulant medicine from leeches ground into powders. "Hair of the dog," Mr. Grant had joked. And Lorin had confided that he wanted to go into medical work someday. He already had a college credit, and, when he spoke, Dad said, he had the saddest authority he'd ever heard from a boy talking to his elders.

Much, much later, I would find myself, a college girl, shouting at my father, "They didn't know enough to take a boy like that to a shrink!" Our fight was no doubt about something else. Later I sought Dad out to apologize and he wasn't there. And so I never had a chance to tell him what, in calming down, I suddenly came to see I must tell him.

On the Monday following the incident with Lorin, when I arrived at the cafeteria with my class, I heard none of the other classes singing their songs, because they'd been instructed to wait for Camfort's group. For years the moment was eclipsed by the full rubber glove and the nightmare of it, which the very next day began to be something we were not to tell others, because some people didn't know how to deal with such things.

There we stood in the cafeteria, all of us, listening to the cashier — the man who was head of Food Services — try to explain to the whole Pompano Beach Grammar School that from now on we would do a single school blessing all at once at twelve-thirty. He said he didn't know about us, but he, for one, was troubled by the inconvenience our old tradition was causing the serving ladies. He'd discussed the problem with the principal and been given permission to introduce one blessing. It made a lot more sense.

However, this man continued, we were not to think he hadn't observed the way we'd been acting sacrilegiously during the singing of other blessings not our own. Last Friday our little game had caused an incident that had been the worst thing ever to happen in his cafeteria. It was an outrage, if we knew to what he referred.

"But my dear sir," Mr. Camfort interrupted. His eye mowed down the cashier. "On behalf of these young people I ask you to reconsider your proposal, if we can be inclusive of all that is outrageous." At least he said something like that. I never could imitate, later, his arch turns of phrase.

I suppose few people trusted our teacher's cleverness, and the head of Food Services wasn't about to touch the tar baby now. He decided right then that he would simply ignore Mr. Camfort as best he could. Mr. Camfort was, after all, the silliest person in Pompano Beach.

The head of Food Services then ordered his helpers to pass out the sheets of paper he'd prepared so that we might vote for the blessings we preferred — first, second, third, and fourth. He explained that we could sing them, as one group, one a day in rotation to the end of term.

But how young we were to be invited to read the impressive column of titles our songs made. (There were so many!) Some of the children in the lower grades had never voted with a pencil before and had to be told several times that there weren't enough pencils to go around and that they had to choose quickly and share with their neighbor; some of them had not wanted to share; and all of them were reduced to staring and staring, because they had no facility to make such a decision quickly and were struck by the confusion of the many little boxes in which to put an X or a checkmark. Which mark did he want? Hands went up. They didn't read very well, some of them, so the teachers hurried around and around the tables, bending and helping until, in all corners of the gigantic room, a great clamor arose which we older ones noticed when we were finished and sat waiting for all the young ones who were going to take forever. And so my classmates and I sat there for a while with just enough extra time for our private in-tuitions, full of foreboding and full of dread, that there was going to be a kind of lambent dullness in the world to come. And more wars.

IN A
SWEET WEEK OF
DYING

IN POMPANO we knew people still raising brawny
Hereford and eggplant and Best Boy tomatoes the size of
softballs. But the wealthy members of our new congregation there turned out to be the orchid growers, Mr. and
Mrs. Fulmore, whose daughter was hit by a truck out on
US 1 during a four-inch rain. At the funeral my mother
whispered to me across the plain pine pews, "Please take
out that chewing gum and put it in this tissue." The girl,
Julie Ann, lay fragrantly asleep in a bank of flowers named
after her. The orchids were tiny lime ones, the color of
sherbet, and her little gown and pumps were dyed the same
shade.

I had a sidelong view of late-comers — whole families,
conferring at the back of the sanctuary. They looked damp.
Ten ushers with white boutonnieres — all local men, all
experienced and good-natured — bristled to get everyone
seated in time. I watched Mr. MacKay sail out to find room

somewhere for the Garys. He seemed embarrassed that they were thoughtless enough to add so many of themselves to the crowd at the last minute. Everyone craned to watch them, the hangdog Gary children, who knew more about the accident than anyone else. We watched their blond heads bow as if they were all connected to the same neck. The youngest suddenly spoke out. She was five; her whispery voice cracked so we all heard her question: she just wanted to know if that was Julie Ann up there.

Out on their strip of US 1, a dozen Fulmore greenhouses sat row after row on property adjacent to the Gary muck farm. Julie Ann's death made that almost private stretch of highway suddenly compelling. People had been driving out there to gawk the whole week before the funeral, their children lolling over the front seats, watching out for the Australian pines planted as an Atlantic windbreak a generation before. Forty-two on one side of the road, forty-two on the other. I'd counted them. They were several stories high, and looked like spires in a German forest. The Fulmores' hidden drive appeared first and then the Garys'. Coming up quickly at unexpected intervals on that straight road, I would always look first for notches and then the pieces of broken bicycle flasher that distinguished the two drives. Suddenly the whole place became my idea of majestic — a scene worthy of blood and tragedy now that it had happened there, the death of our most elegant child, for whom those same trees would rise up dark green in our minds whenever we thought of her.

Any day of the week my father might announce we were going out after supper to visit one or the other of the two families. The Fulmores and the Garys were the high and the low of our congregation. We would have been hard-pressed to choose. We had our leanings and longings in both directions. Backwoods Gary people were in my father's secret past, though we knew little more now than we ever had known about it. At some point he'd plowed with a mule somewhere and gone bathing in a river and had a brother die of a broken back when a rope broke over some rocks at a swimming hole. We knew about it more from the way Gay Nell Gary sent us home with bags of washed collard greens than from anything that was said. Some-times, all alone, my father would dish up cold collards on a cold plate. He broke cornbread into a glass of milk and ate it with a big soup spoon.

"Hello in there," my mother would call, sounding just like an old shoe as soon as we pulled up in the Garys' yard, not far from where three tire swings hung down like the loops on window shades. I was getting old enough to know it was not natural for my mother to be cupping her hands like that and calling out, "Are you *in* there? Are you hiding?"

"Caroline!" It was always Gay Nell from deep down in her house. "Caroline!" And out she'd come, fat but limber for the occasion. She had good reason to believe my mother was an angel. "You look so pretty. If you hadn't stopped in soon, I was going to tell on you."

It was a joke — the notion of Gay Nell complaining and getting us moved. My father's appointments were humble, but they were always handed down by a Methodist bishop headquartered in Lakeland, at the small church college whose most recent buildings were designed in 1936 by Frank Lloyd Wright. Gay Nell Gary wouldn't have had any reason to know the details, but the famous architect had listened to my own mother play the *Moonlight* Sonata one Sunday afternoon, standing in her dormitory foyer not ten feet from her, wearing what she thought she remembered as spats.

Mother loved to tell the story to Norma Fulmore, who pretended to suffer every time she heard it. It was a friendly comic despair. She said the greatest *wrong* to Florida Southern College was Mr. *Wright*. Fifteen years had gone by, she said, and his buildings still looked, in her estimation, like something built by Martians.

We believed that Norma Fulmore was untempted by her money. She insisted her family travel. They brought home art. Once they'd brought home an original painting by the man who'd designed the seal for UNICEF. At the same time she could appreciate her neighbors, whose style was more or less in having a ready can of cashews on the table. "Have some! Come on, have some!" Gay Nell might exclaim, especially to a guest like Norma Fulmore. "Daddy! Pass Norma the nuts!"

I was starting to appreciate the unlikelihood of someone like Norma Fulmore politely helping herself from that can. She was not high and mighty, and I'd watch her give her attention over to Mr. Gary, though he would start up a shocking story before the can had even gotten around the room. If anything, I'd wish that Mrs. Fulmore wasn't there so the story could be enjoyed more freely. One time when Mr. Gary was a boy, he and his cousins had caught live rats to take over to a Mr. Wilcox's place to feed a teenage-size alligator the old man kept in his bathtub. "Of all the carrying-on," Mr. Gary said, recalling the alligator trying to catch that rat inside a slippery tub. He was a laconic man. In one sentence he'd have hoisted up a bloody scene — the smeared porcelain walls, the thwacks of the alligator's tail, and that gang of splattered boys running down the uncarpeted stairs to go get another rat. "Every time we come back with his dinner, Mr. Wilcox would call out, 'Go on up, boys! You know where he is. Go on up there. I'm tired.' "

My father would be smiling to himself by now, and poor Gay Nell would be looking as if she feared this story had crossed some invisible line.

"Well, honestly," she'd say, "where in heaven's name was his *wife* all this time?"

"What's that?"

"His WIFE! Mr. Wilcox's WIFE!"

"Oh, she didn't ever go up there with us." Mr. Gary pretended to have misheard. "Wasn't interested!"

Norma Fulmore would catch my eye and wink. She somehow made me pull in and take shallow, dignified breaths the way my mother did when we had a turn at the other household. Mom would pull herself a little higher in her chair for most of the evening. She didn't try to perfect Norma's posture, but she partook of the genre.

"Look at this beautiful book Julie Ann picked out at an antique store in London," Norma Fulmore would say after a formal meal at her linen table. She served fresh fish terrines and the lightest biscuits with seasoned butter. Her roast gravy smelled of fragrant, illegal wines.

"Oh," my mother said as she was passed the book in the candlelight that showed off everyone's hands, "what a beautiful thing."

"But here's what is so startling about it," Norma Fulmore said, and on that particular visit we learned about rare endpapers in children's books. Norma Fulmore was a small collector.

"Isn't it beautiful, girls? Girls?"

Our mother feared we'd inherited Dad's inability to muster enthusiasm for something that, in all honesty, was not very interesting to him. In polite conversation he was often found to be not listening. ("Noel . . . Noel?")

After dinner, Graham Fulmore liked to disappear with my father out to the greenhouses for a chat — a Methodist version of a brandy and cigar without the stimulants. Later they'd come back with a shallow box of Mr. Fulmore's best hybrids for Mom to take home. He'd have fitted each stem in its own stoppered beaker, slenderer than a pencil. They looked to Jeanie and me like delicate vials for perfume, and we kept the empty ones secreted in a drawer with our scarves. The vials held an assortment of corsage pins I sometimes took to the window, counting and re-counting the pearlized heads.

"Put these in your refrigerator, Caroline," Norma Fulmore would say, making a presentation of a whole box of white orchids surrounded by the larger violet ones with the yellow-and-red throats. Norma said she never had anything *else* homemade to send back with us. "Put those in with your vegetables," she'd whisper to Mom, giving her a light pat through the window of the car. She was a size-six woman who wore earrings for every day and a heavy ring that looked as if it were about to ripen. I was always on guard to catch it in midair, a deep green birthstone set with small diamonds and seed pearls.

"So many?" Mom would say. Sometimes their eyes watered as if they weren't going to see each other for a year. "You're being extravagant."

"Well, someone has to spoil you."

The enormous orchids rode into town on my mother's lap. Their sculpted petals trembled with the ordinary movements of the car, my mother breathing lightly for their sake and for the sake of the thing she held in her lungs — the style. When we pulled into the parsonage driveway she might have to let it all out again. "Mr. Parks is here," she'd say, with good cheer, as we climbed out of the car, taking the box of orchids so that she could hug an elderly man whose stubby whiskers shone like mica. He was our retired plumber come to tinker with the old works of the parsonage, free of charge.

"Sweetheart, I hear we got us another leak."

But on Sunday Mom would wear one of the orchids right in its little glass vial. They were being shipped this way all over the country the spring Julie Ann was squashed on the highway, running, with nymph's arms few girls possessed at her age, to meet the Gary children.

Everyone remembered where he was when he first heard about the death. First we heard it was a station wagon, then a milk truck; one version had it that it was the school bus itself; she was crossing the highway to walk down to the billboard where the kids waited every morning. That story had its holes, though. Why would she do *that* when Julie Ann attended Miss Laurel's private academy and rode daily in a car clear to Lantana in the other direction? The stories were revised all the rest of the week, everyone trying to account for why it had been the Fulmore child and not one of the Gary kids, running back and forth on that wet road like rabbits.

.   .   .

They were a small pack. The Garys took me and my sister
on exhausting hikes when we visited — a different route
every time through the woods or across an unirrigated field
to the sulphur lake, where they fished for bream and
scooped up small fiddler crabs the size of quarters. They
held fiddler crab wars in the bottom of tin cans. They liked
to kick the ground for quail eggs to give to their dogs.
Jeanie would come back with hives and have an asthma
attack by nightfall. Georgia, their oldest, who supposedly
never said a word, started staying back at the farmhouse
with Jeanie when we visited, lighting a kerosene lamp and
leading the way to the attic, where, Jeanie claimed, the girl
actually *talked*. That left me with all the boys, though there
was the tiny girl, the baby. It wasn't the baby but a boy
called Hark who used to wait up for me when I got behind.
"Are yew comin', are yew comin'?" He had a patient grin
and huge pink-and-black gums just like a cat's.

But after dinner at the Fulmores', Jeanie and I would sit
with Julie Ann outside in a wooden swing that held the
three of us bunched together like a trio of rag dolls, though
Julie Ann and I would eventually go off to play. Unobserved, I could do quite well playing with her, even when
she looked tied up like a package, the wide satin sash
around her waist matching the smocking on the bodice of
her dress. She wasn't spoiled; she didn't presume. Soft-
spoken, as unsure of me as I was of her, she'd point out to
me the better features of her doll house — the unglued logs
in the fireplace, the ormolu on the fixtures of the lamps.
Sometimes her father would seek us out for a moment,
attempt to make us laugh by squatting with great difficulty
and looking bug-eyed at us through one of the doll house
windows — poor, eager, loving, sad, and unfortunate Mr.
Fulmore.

"Turn around!" Julie Ann had said to him on the morning of the accident. "I don't want them to see you." The Gary children were gathered down by the billboard waiting for the bus, shouting to each other as they threw little rocks up at the billboard picture. They were always trying to hit the camel square in the yellow head. Some mornings Georgia waved when she saw Julie Ann arrive at the spot where their drive met the highway — and to Mr. Fulmore, lingering with his daughter while they waited for the car from Miss Laurel's.

But that morning in the heavy rain, Georgia may have waved more urgently than usual above the Garys' high, unanimous thrill at being soaked. Georgia had waved and waved as the rest of them, shrieking, collapsed on one another and seemed to roll around drunk. And she kept on waving this time, as if she could see Julie Ann had on a new raincoat, or maybe she kept waving because of the drama of the rain. Something. Julie Ann told her father flatly that she wanted to cross over there for a minute. For a minute only to show Georgia her raincoat.

"All right," Mr. Fulmore said, taking her arm.

"Turn around!" she told him. "They'll think I'm a baby."

"All right," he said, amused, seeing nothing was coming, checking in both directions a couple of times, before turning his back and walking (*hmm tee dum*) away, looking up at the sky like Pooh Bear being a good sport. "Go ahead," he'd said, strolling off to wait for her. He deliberately turned his back to satisfy her pride. "Run along," he called, laughing.

And coming up from Miami, a pale blue pickup truck without its lights on sped into that dark straight cut of trees like a soda rocket.

.   .   .

That was all Jeanie and I were told at the time. We were older and living in other Florida towns before we heard how Mr. Fulmore had sat in the road with Julie Ann while they waited for the ambulance, and that he'd moaned aloud and buried his face in her hair. The old parishioners from the Pompano church would sometimes look us up on their way back from their vacation trips to Mammoth Cave, and that story came up again and again: how the driver of the pickup had had to stand guard over Mr. Fulmore and the child so they wouldn't get hit again! Mr. Fulmore couldn't hear anyone talking to him for almost twenty minutes.

From the souvenir shops at Mammoth Cave the old parishioners used to bring Jeanie and me candy cigarettes as a joke and, much later, those road-sign pillows for teenagers — SOFT SHOULDERS, DANGEROUS CURVES. Mr. Fulmore had sat there on the highway with his legs straight out, holding and rocking. He sounded like the man in *Gone With the Wind,* which Jeanie read from start to finish in two separate summers. She told me the man in that novel sat with his daughter for days and days.

Whoever took the Gary children home after the accident had made them all join hands. They formed a long string and were led away — a band of peasants who'd been made to witness the stoning of a princess. Someone else remembered driving out to the greenhouses an hour later, and by then a doctor was trying to give Graham and Norma Fulmore a shot of Demerol.

Even without these details, I'd been sick at the thought of having to see Mr. Fulmore and his wife again. Ever again. I feared what such an event might have done to them. Their house, their orchids, their smell — the fragrant soaps I'd tried in all the bathrooms — wouldn't provide any shelter. I longed to attend the funeral, to view and memorize the body, but it was a terrifying idea to think of Norma Fulmore seeing me in church. Alive for no reason.

That week while we waited, my mother often touched my head or held me against her. This made me lonely in my knowledge. What was causing me to appear so sorrowful was this: I knew that when Julie Ann's mother would be led into the church right past where I was sitting, and when she floated by, with her kind ashen eyes and crushed hands, a woman in her state, kindred to a ghost, would have the power to look right through a person.

At school the day before the funeral, I stood in a long line with my classmates waiting for a polio shot, and suddenly felt a voice cry out as I saw that the head and tail of our line were not in communication. In her lesson on the dinosaurs, Miss Brice had just explained that such a phenomenon could lead to extinction. Extinction was slow and evolutionary, she'd explained, giving this information without meaning to confound our new awareness that extinction was quick. The thwack of a tail.

Julie Ann.

Her body had obsessed us all week because there'd been confusion in many families as to whether or not children should be taken to see her at the funeral home. But only I was shameless enough to have an image of a bloody bathtub being washed down by a gang of boys. The tub had been in my mind all week. Now, standing in line outside the school nurse's office, I began to sob, looking ahead and behind and seeing that neither head nor tail of the line was visible. Marlene had been at the front when we'd filed out, and I knew she probably had her arms wrapped around the school nurse while the visiting doctor gave her the shot. This was sixth grade. I was practically grown. I tried to think about this, but it was too late; I'd attracted the attention of Miss Brice. There she was, wanting kindly to know why I was crying. She had the good sense to take me out of the line for a moment. Was I frightened? she suggested. Was it Julie Ann?

I looked and told the truth. "I'm going to become a missionary," I said.

Miss Brice was young. I saw her turn bright red, trying to think what she should do if one of her youngsters was having a religious experience. I would have spared her this if I could. She and I had no idea what to do except wait for her to be quick on her feet.

"Well, I know one thing," Miss Brice ventured, finally. She put a new matter-of-factness in her high, thin voice. "You'll have to have a lot of shots if you're going to be a missionary. They need more shots than anyone."

And then I felt her put a hand on my shoulder to steady us both for a few moments while our dinosaur inched closer to the door of the clinic and she could leave me to take my turn hugging the nurse. I didn't feel the needle go in. I only heard the visiting doctor congratulate me; this was the last one in the series, he explained, and he wanted to thank us for being in the experiment. On my way past the lady at the table station I was handed a campaign button. It said POLIO PIONEER. And when I'd put the button on my sweater out in the hall with the other children, whom Miss Brice had asked please to use their indoor voices, I wasn't sure if God's still small voice had been real or imagined. I felt a hollowness that reminded me simply of an empty stomach. But I knew this might be what strong conviction felt like as it dropped out of a person unprepared to receive it.

Many are called but few are chosen.

They didn't play organ music at the funeral home. The individual viewing chapel was a soundproof chamber where the body lay under light coming from indirect sources. Since the walls and floors were dark blue, Julie Ann looked as if she were being displayed on velvet. Her height, like my own, had been average and undramatic. But the body in repose achieved an agonizingly tiny length — Julie Ann, diminished by the bank of pale yellow green. I don't know where people had heard it, but it was in everyone's whisper as they stared: the hybrid orchid had, in a matter of days, been officially named "the Julie Ann." Permission, too, was granted to use lipstick and rouge. In that privilege alone she sailed completely out of Jeanie's and my world. Nothing could compete with it. The brushed-out shining hair, the folded fingers, the stained cheeks.

Along with my mother's corsage, two girls' corsages arrived at the parsonage for Jeanie and me to wear to the funeral, and before I went to bed I opened the refrigerator and studied mine through the cellophane — the Julie Anns, trembling and small, the size of silver dollars. Many are called, few are chosen. For girls the call always landed us in the mission field, away from civilization. In my mind I'd seen it as a very literal field of weeds and high waving sawgrasses, in which insects hopped around the tough dark legs of the natives all day long, until the sun set and we all picked up the camp-stools and slate tablets and went back to a thatched village. I took out cold milk and my mother's pudding. All that changeless sunlight and all those long years, reciting the alphabet with grown men and women whom I knew privately to be as sweet and unfulfilling as orphans in a Home. The idea made me lonesome before I'd even started, and I felt the full despair of my human frailty then. I knew I was not immune to the torpor of privilege and laziness that had spread like a cloud over the world.

The next day Julie Ann was moved to her final public viewing place in our church sanctuary — just behind the altar railing, just below my father's pulpit. There, the light was ordinary, even paltry, so that the beauty of the child was the more startling; she was radiant all by herself.

But by then everyone was exhausted. When the head usher finally closed the coffin, we saw we would get through the sad occasion after all, though there'd be little way to keep from weeping buckets. Sobs had already started up, because the soft organ hymns were full of direct messages heard only at a time like this. Red-eyed men acknowledged one another openly, nodding over the heads of their families.

Then we all seemed to see at once that we were not going to be noticed by Julie Ann's parents. Norma and Graham Fulmore stepped out from the choir room of the church flanked by relatives who'd been secluded with them. A small group of total strangers filed out to take seats in the first three pews, cordoned off with ribbons. I looked up to receive an indifferent glance from a slender, well-dressed woman, who didn't know me from Adam. Her eyes went straight through me and saw nothing. In solemn attendance was a set of youngish grandparents and four or five distinguished-looking men without wives who people guessed were business associates. The whole Pompano congregation stiffened at the expensive black veils, the conservative suits. In our collective shame we were confused past all grieving during the rest of the service.

Sometime in the late afternoon, the parsonage got very quiet and the rain finally stopped. When Jeanie and I heard our parents' bed squeak, Jeanie shot me a look that made us throw down our books and run outside so we could burst with embarrassment.

" 'You're not just a bird turding,' " Jeanie said, imitating Mr. Gary. It was his favorite expression, which no one could break him from saying around us, not even Gay Nell. "You're not just a bird turding," he loved to say to anyone who had spoken some admirable truth.

Jeanie and I had sealed ourselves inside the closed car out in the driveway so that they wouldn't hear us carrying on. Soon Jeanie had stretched out on the back seat and was lying down, feeling her head. "I'm running a fever," she said with surprise. Suddenly she sounded like Mom, asking me to feel how hot she was and then reaching out to touch my head to measure a difference. She said, "I guess I'm coming down with something."

After supper Dad drove us out to check on how the Garys were doing, because all the attention had been on the Fulmores. Dad said the Garys must just now be feeling the aftershocks.

I hung over the front seat and waited for the height of those pines to show, for the road to darken and thread itself between them. Julie Ann was in the ground now. Too soon. I had a rush of wishing all this could somehow last, this loud hum or buzz to the car, this whirring out on the road and in everything we did — all of it brighter in this sweet week of dying. The steady nose-point of the car holding the road and the late colors of the sun, breaking up, streaking the sky, seemed to make the blood in my head sing praises. I was as wrung out as an old dishrag, as if I'd spent the past days and nights carousing on a boardwalk. And still I wanted to pump my arms wildly to keep it all going. I think I knew then that, as soon as all this was over, my hopes, my mission field in the tall sawgrass, would shrink to a quick movement of some exotic wing catching the light before disappearing over the horizon. Or it might never disappear quite. It might stay out there my whole life, turning like a piece of foil caught in a tree where I could see it once in a while, sending little signals to me with every gentle, stupid gust of breeze. I was a weak sort of person, I saw that now, like most people.

The Gary boys sat in the living room giving each other looks. They would kill each other if any one of them made a face. "She was called home," Gay Nell began, too theatrically. I hated to see the unreserve of farm people dragging itself out in front of everyone. "We can get the call any time, that's for sure," Gay Nell began again, but then wailed, and there were teeth and spittle showing when she tried to whisper her next thought: "But she was too little an angel, now wasn't she?"

I saw Mom move to the couch beside Gay Nell while Dad and Mr. Gary both stood together, silent, dying those thousand deaths.

Mom's head shot up when Dad cleared his throat, a nervous habit. The boys looked as if they *would* crack up then, fending off laughter with mean stares of accusation; they'd get whipped after, if they ever did such a thing while the preacher was there.

Later, Dad sat beside me and took my temperature and put a green cloth on my head with bits of ice he'd crushed with a hammer we kept in our kitchen drawer. For a man it was easy, I thought, looking at him wrap the ice. Men were assigned to churches. Men weren't all sent off to Africa the way we were.

"I guess you have the flu," he said, smiling. I felt like a person being airlifted out of a plane crash in the middle of the world's dark continent.

"I keep seeing things," I told him. I wanted to prolong the pleasure of being awake late at night with my father sitting on my bed; I improvised as I went along, the hot fever making it easier. "I keep seeing the rats," I told him.

"What rats?" I felt him move farther onto the bed for balance. "There aren't any rats. You've been dreaming."

"Those rats they gave the alligator. Mr. Wilcox's alligator."

"Oh, that," he said. "You go to sleep now . . . shhh."

"Did you ever hear what happened?" I said, knowing that I *had* to have a regular life; that without one I'd blow away like chaff in the wind. I reached up to keep him there. My father's face and neck were as cool and dry and necessary as drawing breath to live. "Did you ever hear what they did to him?" I said.

"Nope."

"Gay Nell told us they had to shoot him finally."

"Oh, what if they did," he whispered, treating this as some nonsense put in our heads. "Gay Nell wasn't even there at the time," he whispered; "she was still a schoolgirl, and hardly anyone was born yet." He was thinking he could get me to drift off.

"She said they didn't shoot him in the bathtub."

"I should hope not . . . shhh."

"They put him in the lake and then shot him!" Jeanie called from the other room. She'd been lying there listening through the thin wall.

"Now, that will do!" Dad said.

Gay Nell had told us kids about it in private, when she'd gotten us alone. She had all the details. A few neighbors with dogs and small children got upset when they learned Mr. Wilcox had turned the alligator loose in the lake, where it might accidentally hurt someone. Mr. Wilcox should have taken him somewhere else; but he'd said, no, if he was going to have to give him up (Mrs. Wilcox had finally put her foot down), he wanted him out there where he could walk down to the bank and see him once in a while. But then there was a hue and cry to remove him. None of the boys was allowed to go in to try to drag him out alive, because it was too dangerous. He'd been free and swimming around for over a week.

"A beautiful creature," Gay Nell had claimed, "much more beautiful than you think of them being — plated with armor, with streets and avenues like a gameboard. And then that soft white belly. Tender as a peeled egg."

He'd risen and fallen in the water when the boys shot him, she said. He'd risen and fallen, risen and fallen, right at the old man's feet. Mr. Wilcox was standing there the whole time, seeing what a sorry job they were doing. "Go on, boys!" he'd had to urge them, "Shoot! Shoot him!" It had taken him several days to resign himself to this, Gay

Nell said; he'd burned hot and cold over it, she said, not knowing it was the phrase that would stay to haunt me. I'd been an empty girl filled up for a week, turning hot and cold. I could weep buckets over Julie Ann's tiny green pumps, and run a fever, and swear to die with faith in the Congo, even seeing myself rise and fall in the black water — pitifully coming to the surface several times, or one last time in the dark, pulpy shadows. But all the time another self, whom I also loved, stood up on that bank in a smelly undershirt and work pants, giving in to everything and whining with a kind of sickly odor, hurrying them, urging them, low in the back of my throat, "Go on, boys! Shoot!"

THE
BABOON
HOUR

LONGLY METHODIST in North Jacksonville was
Dad's first city appointment. A year before, a Dino filling
station had sprung up in front of the sanctuary, and when
we'd settled into their parsonage, the people told us they
were still upset by the filling station, but not as much as
they were by the dentist. Longly Methodist had lost
twenty families to him. He hadn't been coming to the services more than six months, they said, before he began
holding prayer vigils right in his own home.

It had started with a woman with cancer who had small
children and a frantic husband. The dentist told the husband all the church had to do was pray without ceasing. It
had seemed a small enough thing to ask until the man and
a few families began to wear themselves out because the
rest of the congregation hadn't gone along with it. Toward
the end, everyone got a call and an angry Bible verse
quoted into the telephone — "God forbid I should sin

against Him in ceasing to pray!" People felt sick over the misunderstanding and dreaded the phone ringing night or day. "What ye desire when ye pray *believe!*" Or, "Morning and evening, will I pray and cry aloud and He shall hear my voice!" The previous minister hadn't known how to handle the situation.

"It's a young couples' church," the president of our Official Board explained to Dad. "We needed us a younger man."

"I don't know when I stopped feeling younger," Dad said. "Just now, I think."

We'd landed in a peeling, sapless neighborhood, putting its hopes in a shopping center. But from the parsonage we could walk to the St. John's River, to the pogy plant on the near bank. Pogy fish were invisible, we were told — little slivers of nothing, little bitty things they caught by the ton and ground into fertilizer. The Jacksonville Zoo, advanced and experimental, sprawled on the other side in a heartening array of humane cages. Self-foraging peacocks roosted on the hurricane fence over there, and some of our parishioners nearby could hear the zoo's two lionesses roaring at night.

We were cut off by our Sunday school building, rising up a few inches from our noses as we stood at the sink doing dishes. Pale pink cinder block. I believed we'd finally arrived, to be living that way behind concrete, hearing the noise of city buses on their way deep into town. Semitrailers honked at us all summer long as they passed our corner, going north and south. They were hauling quiet white-face cattle and decks of red Chevrolets. Riding backward for good luck.

In the evenings we'd get knocks on our door and find a shy migrant worker standing there saying he was on his way to pick apples in North Carolina and peaches on the way back. He needed money. Even his car appeared shy and would shrink back from us if we glanced beyond the man's shoulder out to the curb, where everyone else in the family had a face that was caved in. I could never decide which one was the wife. Teenagers younger than I passed infants back and forth over the seat. They all had moon-round faces and flat platinum hair. In rural towns like Boynton and Ochopee they stayed clear away from people, dotting the groves in the daytime, retreating at night inside barrack housing with dull tin roofs. But here the men seemed experienced. They didn't mind telling us: they needed gasoline. Their frankness excited me. I couldn't wait to start school.

Toward the end of summer, my anticipation turned to self-absorption. I believed I was getting elephantiasis. My grandmother's sister Mary had contracted it when she was my age. Our brittle medical dictionary said, "Most common in tropical regions." A three-inch paragraph zigged and zagged around an etching of a pair of thick legs and a man's swollen genitals. Grandma's sister had only been slightly stricken, from what I could tell from a photograph, taken in 1922, showing her with Grandma after church. Her legs looked like telephone poles standing in concrete, splaying open the tops of her unlaced shoes and ruining, Grandma said, every pair she owned. A blind man had asked for Mary's hand when she was sixteen. He'd never seen anything but swatches of bright blue sky, and by the time Mary finished teachers' college, he was long dead.

My mother agreed I had large ankles. But I was big-boned, she said; I was going to be tall, I was putting on whole inches at a time. It wasn't until the end of August that she figured out what was wrong with *her,* as impossible as it might be, forty-five years old, with thyroid trouble and sciatica. She was much farther along than she could believe, and the sheer prospect was embarrassing. Dangerous, my sister Jeanie told me confidentially. Older women like Mom, in the change of life, had mongoloid babies with big almond eyes as far apart as gills. Poor change-of-life babies. We'd read the Dale Evans story, *Angel Unaware.*

Mom had had plenty of trouble when she was younger. Grandma had once held her hands to show Jeanie and me how our mother's pelvis was no bigger than that. I'd weighed ten pounds and had my head turned wrong. The doctor said I'd more or less tried to shoulder my way out and was too long for him to back up and start over. After me, Mom had had to be trussed up and sent away for a rest. To North Carolina, to Mrs. Barker's guest house, Grandma said, where whenever they painted the porch they mixed in a lot of sand to keep the old ladies from falling off.

Mom drove herself from Jacksonville all the way back to Pompano to see her old doctor, who'd been treating her for a goiter. He'd snapped his fingers when she told him she was pregnant. Did he forget to tell her? he said. The thyroid treatments were hormonal! How could he have forgotten, he said, not looking at her, willing to admit that maybe this was his fault. No one was ever going to talk about suing; he'd gone ahead and snapped his fingers, remembering he hadn't warned her. And it must have sounded to Mom like her own backbone popping at the moment of conception — popping as sweetly as a knuckle.

Something might have been done, we realized later. At the time, though, only spontaneous abortions were within our ken, manageable in my mother's daydreams. Even those, the natural ones, seemed like spontaneous combustion — too rare to hope for — those accidents of happy-go-lucky negligent people who leave turpentine and old rags sitting together in a box.

She worried about Dad. She worried about the private thoughts of his new parishioners, on whom her graciousness had barely taken hold. She had to be careful not to confide in people trying to get close to her, wanting to acquaint her with their church enemies as soon as possible.

A few plump couples started coming by regularly with plates of cookies and very old stories about the dentist era. He had a storefront now, they said, with a growth chart on the back wall that was supposed to be a red thermometer's temperature shooting up as he raised more money. It looked more like a big beaker of blood. The dentist had been real charismatic, they said, rolling their eyes. "Handsome? Boy howdy, he was sure handsome!"

None of these couples were designed for friendship. Too kind and leisurely, too good-hearted and presumptuous, they all wanted to know where we put our heads at night. Where were we all sleeping anyway? Which one had taken the sleeping porch? If Mom had told any of them a truly personal piece of information, she would have scared them half to death.

So she began waking up at night, listening to my bones crack. I put on three inches in a matter of months. She'd hurry to my bedroom, imagining all my femurs and tibias pulled to the brink, but would merely find me curled up. A jumbo shrimp. Had that crack come from the womb instead? I never remembered a thing the next morning, but to her eye my toothbrush would appear smaller in my hand, my slip would have climbed to another high-water mark on my thigh. Still immature, uncompanionable, I towered over the ironing board and pressed wrinkles out of dresses that would have swallowed her up. I still moped around after school that fall, still sang to myself and spent a lot of time breaking into the vacant house next door. When I found a cache of *Playboy* magazines moldering in the attic over there, I brought them straight to her.

"Just throw them in the garbage," she said.

I ran my hand over the top of the stack, inside which lay the balloony breasts of girls looking straight into the camera. "Shouldn't we burn them?" I said.

"I'm way too tired for that," she said, sitting down. Her legs were already aching. "Already." She laughed. "Can you imagine?" And in the middle of the night, she prayed, dear God, that she wouldn't become a fearful person. The mail still brought her mother's letters. Their pages, front and back, warned us of the Last Days, pointed out the Signs of the Times.

In late October my new school instructed me to bring ten pounds of canned food in a canvas bag with my name ironed on it somewhere. My homeroom teacher apologized for the inconvenience, but it was required by the state Board of Education: they were being mindful of the Cape.

Cape Canaveral.

Ground Zero of the South.

Someone in civil defense was experimenting with partial

evacuation should a nuclear disaster happen during school. They picked Longly High because the railroad bed ran behind our sports field. With planning, a freight train could ship us, homeroom by homeroom, across the state line to Georgia. To safety.

"What kind of food do you girls want in your sacks?" Mom said, a little dreamily. She studied the mimeographed sheets we'd brought home one afternoon. She had a ravenous appetite now, but we could see her trying to show a low-keyed interest. In her effort to think evenhandedly of ten pounds of food inside something sturdy, like canvas, she missed the big picture of evacuation.

"Vienna sausages might be good," she said, trying to imagine them, one of her favorite foods, trying to do it right, because the experts had asked her to pack us an interesting lunch, once and for all.

She lay in Dad's BarcaLounger, holding the mimeo sheets at arm's length. On top of everything else, her eyes had suddenly changed overnight to those of a middle-aged woman. What we were to see for the remaining months was Mom lying in that chair, trying to read and tipping herself farther back as she got farther along.

"What's that?" Dad said, seeing her squint. He took the mimeo from her and gave her, instead, a box of letters he needed us to fold and stuff for him. The other box, with the envelopes, needed stamps. And here *they* were, he said, cheerfully — four rolls of stamps he'd picked up at the post office.

"How about canned brown bread?" Mom said. "And they're going to need something to open it all with. Can openers. Good ones."

That night, while he attended an Official Board meeting, Mom and Jeanie and I sat watching *Playhouse 90,* licking stamps in a kind of triple trance and slowly pressing them in place, one by one. Except that we had accidentally turned the box around, so that the envelopes were upside down. When we looked, the stamps were glued in the wrong corners of two hundred addresses. We held up envelope after envelope, but every stamp was in the lower left, looking utterly preposterous. Mom was so upset she pounced at the TV and yanked the cord out of the wall.

Dad came in from his meeting a few minutes later, to find us girls powerless and Mom out of control. Huge cauldrons of water sat simmering on the stove. She was going to steam the stamps off and wouldn't even look at Dad when he came in and told her it didn't matter.

"What do you mean? *Look* what we *did.*"

"They'll go through the mail that way, Caroline. It doesn't matter where you put the stamp. I promise you!"

Mom stopped in the middle of the kitchen, listening to the four big pots hissing just under a boil. "I don't believe you," she said. Her tender mouth trembled fearfully. "I'm so ridiculous-looking," she said, suddenly, looking down at herself. "Oh, Noel."

There was no way to comfort her except for Dad to take her upstairs and put her to bed.

During our first nuclear-disaster drill, the whole school spread out shoulder to shoulder for a march to the railroad tracks. We looked like volunteers combing the field for a body. "Get back in your homeroom groups," the principal kept pleading with us. "Please walk in your room assignment. Teachers! Call your students together!"

The teachers were no help to him. They'd spread out,

too. They looked just like us, equally small and inconsequential in the tall grass. I continued to trudge on with my individual sack. To my left was a red-headed, bosomy girl as tall as I and more solid, who seemed to want to introduce herself. She had a limp. I feared for a moment I was meeting the school invalid, a needy girl who would latch on to me for the rest of the year.

But it was her shoes, she said; they were hurting her. She made a practical speech about putting loafers in with our canned goods if we did this very often. Her name, she said, was Robin Beale. Then she more or less put her cards on the table by telling me outright that her best friend for years — Gina — had moved to Gainesville over the summer with her father. Robin was envious, she said; Gina's father was the kind of man who'd let his daughter buy night creams and mudpacks, not knowing what she needed and what she didn't.

Our friendship might have been sealed on that image of Gina's privileged life. Recently I'd shoved a bar of perfumed soap in with Dad's groceries when he wasn't looking. He'd spread out his items in all innocence for the checker to ring up while he stood smiling, not caring in the least about the soap and perhaps having thoughts about the cold war. Still, it had been a little like stealing from him.

My mother would have picked up the soap and smelled it with appreciation. "You don't believe in things like this, do you?" she would have said, handing it back so I could put it wherever I'd found it. Mom believed in good hair, simple lines, light make-up; but the endless variations, the waste of time in playing with them, filled her with doubt. For her, sin was a measure of one's silliness, and people's extravagances shocked her more than their reputed lusts, though her own husband would not have known what in the world she was talking about. None of this was in Dad's theology.

I felt sorry for Mom now, alone all day in the BarcaLounger, frightened into a kind of numbness. She wasn't herself. When she'd asked what I wanted for my canvas sack, I could have said "I want mudpacks"; I could have shouted "Prince Matchabelli!" and she wouldn't have heard. Things were that bad.

"My mother's pregnant," I blurted out to this large girl walking beside me in the sports field.

For a long time we didn't go to each other's house. We were cautious. Neither of us wanted to get stuck with the other if she turned out to be an utter sad sack. One of the untouchables. During afterschool hours, I wondered if I was too old for friends now, what with my mother upset and coming to *me* when she found Billy, our ancient parakeet, finally keeled over dead in the bottom of his cage. She'd fallen asleep in her chair in the time it took me to find an old sock to put Billy in. Perhaps before this change, I might have buried him with a secret ceremony. Now I put him quietly in the garbage. I found an old sock for him and then an empty shoe box and some heavy rubber bands. Before she woke up I'd taken it all out to the big cans by the curb.

Jeanie showed me an article in *Reader's Digest* called "Baby Weeks," which she cut out with a razor blade close to the binding so that no one would be able to tell pages were missing. She said she didn't think Mom should have to know exactly what blessed *week* she was in — the week of the baby's heart, Jeanie whispered, counting them off on her fingers, the week of its little brain, the week of its little spinal cord. For Pete's sake, she said, we'd all be nervous wrecks.

One day Dad wanted to go to the grand opening of the shopping center, and we noted his forced enthusiasm — as if he were trying to turn back the clock. The four of us piled in the car together, pretending we were eager to see, at eight P.M., a stunt man dive from a ladder into a small tank in the new, bannered parking lot. Mom's perkiness was painful. Oh, she'd had a long nap, she was looking forward to it.

"I guess they think anybody can direct traffic," Dad said when we got within a mile. He rested his head on the steering wheel while high school boys tried to wave cars forward one length at a time. Dad could have done a U-turn and taken us back home, but he looked like a man for whom one thing over another didn't make a difference. He was stunned by the escalation of our problems. It was going to have to be a Caesarean birth, they'd found out that morning. Doctors had consulted and agreed. All signs indicated the baby would be too big for her this time. A Caesarean required a spinal tap, which left some women paralyzed. He and Mom would have to sign a sheaf of paper absolving everyone.

Beside him on the front seat, Mom put her head back and closed her eyes.

"Isn't there a pillow back there?" my father said.

"It's in the trunk, Daddy," Jeanie whispered. The way she patted his shoulder Jeanie suddenly looked twenty years old.

Cheerleaders passed out popcorn to people sitting on their car hoods, under the roving searchlights that found and crossed each other, stupidly, in the dark. It was obvious to people the show wouldn't start on time. The stunt man was supposed to delay his dive so more announcements could be made. A teenage boy kept practicing drum rolls until it became funny to the crowd, and the manager made the kid put his snare on the ground.

Finally the cheerleaders were called forth. The search-lights were demotorized, at last, and trained on the tank during the drum roll. Mom was stretched out on the front seat with her head under the steering wheel, and we were all glad she wasn't watching when the man set himself on fire and dove, head first.

The cheerleaders had joined hands and formed a circle around the tank to show how small it was — only one girl deep and six girls around.

I was glad when it worked out with Robin and we became friends, gradually exclusive at lunchtime, identified more or less as "besters." She was an attractive girl, almost in the extreme. Her mother bought her well-made adult clothes — worsteds and mohairs — which turned Robin Beale into an oddball without her really understanding why. Not so odd that I couldn't be proud of her, but she could have used someone more sophisticated than I was to tell her to tone it down. In five minutes she could have been more popular. I didn't really deserve her.

She claimed her mother had once been a member of our church, and I happened to tell this at supper one night when I was beginning to brag about her. Dad said he'd visit Mrs. Beale in that case. I was sure he would, although it wasn't going to surprise me to find out the woman wasn't interested in us anymore. In this matter I'd achieved some degree of sophistication: Methodism was a matter of taste. Anyone's could change. We'd have been Episcopalian if it hadn't been for John Wesley's experience in his rooms at Oxford, looking down into the byways from his handsome but sparse furnishings and oak-paneled walls. I dreamed I would go to England someday unless I continued to have fat legs, in which case there didn't seem to be much point. In the streets I judged a woman's candidacy for high church and travel by the delicacy of her ankles.

Mrs. Beale's were the most beautiful I'd ever seen: the size of one's wrists.

She had come to the door of the parsonage to meet Mom when she dropped Robin off on a Friday afternoon to spend her first sleep-over. I went to answer the door and there she stood — a small gold woman with hair contours, holding Robin's things on a quilted hanger. The minute Mom saw her and cried out to her, I felt a sensation of tremendous relief: this woman would somehow save us.

"Rachel!" Mom said.

Mrs. Beale was someone Mom had known in college. They hadn't seen each other since, and Mom was embarrassed because her hair wasn't washed and she had on something she was planning to throw out, some polished-cotton maternity thing she tore up the next day for furniture rags. But when they hugged, I saw Mom give in to something. She held Rachel Beale longer than normal and then let herself be led to the couch.

"I haven't told my own mother about this yet," she said, looking down at herself. "She thinks we're living in the Last Days." Mom laughed out loud and hugged Mrs.

Beale again. "Here I am bringing another baby into the world in the Last Days."

They wouldn't have had enough in common to become friends if Robin and I hadn't accidentally thrown them together, crossed their paths that afternoon, made them tell us a few old stories. Mrs. Beale recalled all the details, and Mom just repeated, "Oh goodness, I'd forgotten that." After some hot tea to calm her down, Mom's reserve came back. Her "Oh goodness" — energetic, semiautomatic, developed over a lifetime of plates of cookies — had made my mother too careful for friendship. I thought it close to miraculous when Rachel Beale started coming to see her regularly. I assumed something like divorce must have narrowed the woman's scope. She seemed to have only Robin, whom she slightly overdressed, and a secretarial job; she spoke of an elderly parent up in Raleigh.

But if she was lonely, she didn't seem lonely the way Gwendolyn Helsor did, for example — our adult Needy, standing in the foyer every other day, loaded down with more literature on serious pregnancies than she'd had the last time she'd dropped in on us — more creams and salves, more support hose and succor. "Gwen! We were about to go shopping."

Gwendolyn Helsor would look us all over with suspicion. "Do you think you should?"

"Well, it's hard to keep me home."

The girl's one bad eye was soft and forlorn as it wandered over our furnishings, curious and hopeful, while the good eye continued to stare dead ahead, taking in the truth. "I see," she'd say, preparing to leave. Mom would always break down and tell her to stay and have some cake. It was one thing to be veined and lumpy, with high blood pressure and double sciatica. What if she'd had to be Gwendolyn, as dry and ready for the hearth as a rag rug? The girl's own mother had already given up and deeded her the old family home near the zoo.

Whatever it was Rachel Beale needed from us felt very different from that. It felt like something *we* needed: the women's magazines she brought, for example, and her simple way of ignoring my mother whenever Mom demurred. "I think magazines are real relaxing," Rachel said. "If you don't care for them, you can cut out the coupons."

There was an aristocratic drawl in her voice that didn't jibe with the disturbing way Rachel Beale sat in a chair. The woman's blend of powder and cologne. I couldn't have said what it was at the time — not high-church exactly. There was something of an incongruity in her I'd not seen at such close range — good and bad ideas heaped up on one outfit. If her dresses were subtle, her jewelry was too bangly, too noisy. But somehow all that racket, her "sounding brass or tinkling cymbal," seemed manifestly honest to me; the weathered skin, which I'd associated with hard women, was clean and trustworthy. And no matter how much my mother protested, Rachel just did what she felt like doing and brought magazines.

"They're so expensive," Mom said, smiling, not wanting to be hurtful. "I've never believed in things like this."

"You'll get tips from them," Rachel promised, "all kinds," until Mom began feeling close enough to explain. She'd turn the glossy pages and say she didn't recognize herself or real life in them. It was all advertising.

"Then read the articles. Read the stories!" Rachel could

be as dismissive and joyful as a nurse. "Personally I like the scientific studies they do. Read *them*."

Mom might open her arms then and sigh for whatever it was she lacked in order to appreciate the same things Rachel did. "Well, I guess it's just me," she'd say. And I was embarrassed by her apologetic air, her backing away for the sake of mutual accord, with the lilting regret ("Maybe it's just me"), which sounded a little superior, I thought. I believed that it *was* just my mother. What Rachel Beale had that she lacked was guts.

For a while I thought she seemed Roman Catholic.

One day while Rachel visited she saw someone strolling up to our front door with yet another plate, and she jumped up, fanning the air to disperse her smoke. "I'm slipping out the back, Caroline. If I stay you'll have to put on coffee."

"Oh, don't go," Mom said. "You should stay, Rachel. Nobody's going to bite you."

"I know their stories already," Rachel said. And another time she reasoned that too much of *her* would hinder people trying to get to know us. She began looking in on Mom in the evenings. She said this kept her from colliding with people wanting to visit during the day.

"She's something," Mom said, grateful for this kind of company. She could sit around without stockings, without her make-up or cheerful good looks. And we discovered that the evenings were Mom's gloomy times, when she most needed someone else. It turned out that evening gloominess in primates had been scientifically documented.

"The baboon hour," Rachel Beale explained. She'd read about the phenomenon in a magazine. Anthropologists had made studies of whole families of baboons routinely depressed by the jungle twilight descending on them, saddening them, quite deeply, it appeared.

"Poor things," Mom said.

After a back rub, Rachel would do her own nails or Mom's with cuticle remover or a nail buffer covered with a fine chamois. She especially liked doing Mom's toes. "It's relaxing," she said. So it was surprising when she'd look up from them to tell us another startling piece of information, sometimes on hypnosis or forensic medicine. From her magazines she'd picked up out-of-the-way sociology.

"You know the vinegar the Roman soldiers gave Him on the end of their sword, when He said, 'I thirst'?"

"Yes?"

"It was common knowledge back then that a drop of vinegar would quench the thirst. We're just wrong to think they were being cruel when they were doing Him a favor. It's one of the many things that's been misinterpreted all this time."

I could tell it irked Robin Beale that her mother was becoming so popular with me. At school Robin would hint. I didn't know what it was like to live with Rachel; I didn't have the whole story.

"And you might as well know," Robin threw out one day to trouble the waters, "she hates organized religion worse than anything." As if I cared about organized religion more than regular girls.

"So does my dad," I said. "So do I." I felt cavalier.

"So does your dad *what*?" she said.

"Hate organized religion. They should get married."

When I looked again I was startled to see I'd gotten the best of her. Tears stood in her eyes.

"You wouldn't say that if you knew certain things."

"So what is she, an atheist or something?"

"I could tell you," Robin threatened, getting up to leave, "only I promised her I wouldn't."

Then Robin announced she was sick of me.

I hated seeing a girl of my own ungainly proportions begin to cry, her not knowing in the least how graceless she looked, how blotchy and red her face became. I would be relieved if she stopped coming over to the house with her mother in the evenings. The baboon hours would be better without her. It would be awkward but more manageable if I could remain loyal to Robin by day and crazy about her mother at night. I reasoned Robin had no idea what it was like to have the whole story about *my* mother. "Oh dear, I'll call him, Walter; he's in his study," Mom was always saying when you could see through the open window Dad, in the yard, hitting practice balls with a seven iron. That's what organized religion had done to her. Dad *should* have been married to Rachel. He was the kind of man who'd pick up a receiver and say, "Oh, hello, Walt, I was just out there hitting a few practice balls."

It was Robin I blamed when the next day I was harassed about the old prayer vigil scandal, an assault that came out of nowhere. Robin must have put them up to it — two seventh-graders confronting me at the cold water fountain at school — children of followers of the handsome dentist, followers I thought of as perpetually down on their knees, clenching their fists and throwing back their heads. I never liked even to think of them, though once in a while I imagined the dentist himself, blond and the worst kind of passionate fake; anyone would see through him in a minute. I had to say this for the two girls: they were as brave as terriers.

"We know who your father is," the first one said.

"Who?" I said, but there was no joking with them.

"Your father ought to tell people what the Bible says," the same one continued, nudging her friend, who had clammed up on her. "You're supposed to pray without ceasing. Your father's church just lets people die."

When an enormous bell went off over our heads, all three of us jumped, and the expression on the spokesman's face dissolved. She was relieved this was over.

"Well, bye," she said, smiling, herself again. "See you tomorrow!"

Maybe Robin had thought it funny to send me these messengers. But the joke, if it was a joke, only made her mother the more attractive choice.

"So *is* she an atheist?" I asked Robin at lunch a few days later when she agreed to eat with me. I kept quiet about the seventh-grade girls. Instead, I humbled myself in an effort to get her to talk. Some things about her mother might give me pause, if she'd just tell me what they were. "Is that what she is? An atheist?"

"No," Robin said. She saw what I was up to.

It was quite tantalizing now, the secret she was sworn not to tell. She'd ceased sounding resentful and petty about her mother. At school she was dour and sad. Without my understanding for a while what had happened, I was filled at night with feelings of . . . what? Unconditional love? No secret crime of Rachel Beale too dark for me to forgive? Once I sat at my desk listing everything I could think of, from A to Z. And I could never think of anything, not one thing, that would be impossible to forgive.

Besides, she was funny and a little shocking. The way she talked about her father, for example, the very next evening. Mom had started bleeding; the doctors weren't sure what was going to happen. Rachel was a godsend; we didn't deserve her. She sat telling us stories about her crazy father to keep our minds off ourselves.

One time, at his worst, her father had grabbed an invisible friend, Wilkus, her imaginary playmate, out of her arms and flung him into the ocean. She was only five or six at the time.

"I don't understand," Dad said. "Wilkus was not real? Not a real doll?"

"Utterly imaginary!"

Rachel paused. "I remember my poor mother standing up in the boat, pleading with Daddy not to do it, but he was so angry he just kept raising Wilkus higher and higher over his head. Then he brought him down with all his might."

Rachel's own arms flung the nothing in her hands so hard that we all bent forward and followed her sad gaze into the deep — the imaginary friend cruelly irretrievable.

The idea of a father this violent was horrifying and exhilarating. I had heard no story anything like it.

But then, Rachel said, there were two outrageous things her father had done to woo her mother when they were practically still teenagers. Rachel held up one finger for the first thing: he gave a stack of new dollar bills to a friend who ran a stationery shop and who knew how to gum one end of the stack the way he gummed professional notepads. When the gum dried, you could tear a new dollar bill off the top as if it were just a piece of paper. "Daddy gave the money to my mother as a present. She was supposed to carry it in her purse and take the whole thing out when she wanted to spend a dollar. Everyone in town was talking about her at the end of the week, her coming in with that moneypad. No one believed the money was real." She paused. "Did you ever know a con artist?"

I opened my mouth to ask her if she'd ever met the dentist, but my mother cleared her throat. She didn't approve of gossip at my age. "What was the other thing?" Mom said. "You said there were two things."

The other thing was the time he walked up and down the street in front of her mother's house, holding a fistful of live dragonflies tied to strings, eerily suspended over his head, until he had the neighborhood outside watching him.

"Who wouldn't have wanted to marry him!"

Mom blushed. I wondered if Rachel's secret had been inadvertently spoken: Who wouldn't have wanted to marry *her*? I decided it was something like four or five husbands and boyfriends in between. A messy life. That was nothing difficult to forgive.

But my imagination ran in another direction a few days later, when I stood with Mrs. Shore in our darkened living room while we watched Mr. Shore come in and out with pieces of a white baby crib they wanted us to have so people would know what *not* to get us. If Mom was up to it, the surprise shower was in three weeks.

Mrs. Shore was no longer up to anything, except to boss her husband around. She was seriously ill with cancer, and I saw then how difficult it could be to live with her. "Put those slats against the wall, Walter. I don't want you going upstairs with them. Caroline will think you were snooping in her house while she was asleep. No, no, over *there*! Noel will take care of it when he gets in." Her husband, whipped numb, would see his wife through to the death. But maybe Rachel Beale had abandoned a dying husband, Robin's own father, and run off with someone else. Now *that* was, finally, the worst thing I'd thought of, and I stood waiting for the idea to make a difference to me.

Of course nothing happened. The ability to forgive her was stronger, so much stronger, in fact, that I felt it suddenly for Mrs. Shore herself, standing at my side and looking up at me in alarm. She saw now that I'd been shooting straight up all fall while she'd been shrinking. Which of us was going the fastest — me in one direction or Mrs. Shore in the other? God's unconditional love extended to the woman's very cells, I thought, and was swept by the mystery of such a thing. The cells were said to be doubling and redoubling every day, every minute, and yet they were taking her right down, like locusts taking down a sapling.

During the latter weeks of my mother's pregnancy, the weeks of the baby's fingers and toes and nails and follicles, Mom could get up and about if she was careful. She started walking slowly around the block with Rachel in the evenings, and I was sure Mom learned what the crime was during those sunset strolls. The desire to know the details of it was stronger now. I wanted to be tested by the truth, the real story.

"She's had it very hard" was all Mom would tell me

when I tried to get it out of her. "I keep thinking she'll start coming back to church. But I don't know. It can be impossible for people after a point."

What point? At what point was it impossible? I needed to know. If Rachel was no longer a Methodist or anything organized, and if she wasn't an atheist, then what was she now?

"She's a good person," Mom said, a little taken aback. "A good soul."

But I knew that wasn't it, for Pete's sake.

"An agnostic?" Jeanie offered. "That's what I am, I think."

Nothing could be more disappointing than an agnostic. It challenged nothing, tested nothing.

I was thrown back on my list of adulterous crimes.

She'd begun helping Mom take spit baths at night to prevent an accident that might induce labor. Things were on schedule, the doctors said. They were going to deliver the baby two weeks early. Mom had to take back everything she'd said about magazines, because she was finding herself all over the place now — in the first-person accounts of Caesarean moms, in the prenatal question-and-answer column, in the "Nine Month Quiz Corner" — until one day she discovered she couldn't bend over the sink far enough to wash her hair. Jeanie and I almost called Rachel on the phone. She'd stayed away that night, the night of the surprise shower, and Dad had a meeting. The two of us were responsible for getting Mom over to the church basement on some pretense, and we were dumbfounded when she suddenly declared she was going to bed. We watched her begin climbing the slow stairs.

"Mama," Jeanie said, reluctant to have to break down and tell her the great guarded secret.

"I'm going to bed," she said.

Jeanie went to the banister and held Mom's hand while she told her that every woman in the whole church practically was over there waiting for her.

Mom stared at us in disbelief. "How could you let this happen?"

"They've been planning it since September."

It made us sick to see her sit right down on one of the stairs. She couldn't go over there looking like this, she said. "I'm just not going over there looking like this."

The magazine tip said that if we didn't have the commercial dry shampoo in the house, oatmeal would work. Or even flour, if we brushed it out with at least fifty strokes.

"I looked like I had on a wig," Mom told Rachel when she came the next evening. Hundreds of pink and blue boxes with the tissue hanging out were staircased to the ceiling in the nursery behind a white stuffed lamb.

"Well, they certainly do love *you*," Rachel said, lighting up her cigarette with marvelous disregard. She reached over and picked up a mound of Mom's hair.

"You could have used kerosene on it, too," she said. "Have you ever heard of that? Dry-cleaning your hair with kerosene?"

My mother drew back from her.

"Or gasoline, either one. It takes the oil out, but if you have red in it like you do, it leaves you wild and provocative."

"Well, we didn't have any," Mom said, half laughing, "and we still don't. I don't want to be wild and provocative." We watched Rachel show how Mom's hair would look if she thrilled it with a little treatment of gasoline. She made snaky motions with her hands around Mom's mousy head.

"Not me," Mom said, shooing her away.

The upstairs felt like a girls' dormitory. Jeanie said we should get a bottle of bleach. Dad was downstairs snoring, his novel collapsed on his chest like a sand castle hit by a little wave. Rachel got a chair and put it inside the tub for Mom to sit on while she washed her hair with regular shampoo. None of us had thought of this. I stood in the door and saw Rachel strip to a lacy bra and step inside the tub with Mom, who kept on a housecoat and held the bucket and cup. Had she ever posed for magazines? I suddenly wondered. Was that her crime? I took a quick look at the few places where her good muscles were letting go, admiring her lack of modesty.

"My daddy said if he *ever* caught me kerosening my hair, he'd whip me," Rachel said. "He told me he'd heard of a young girl catching on fire that way."

"How terrible," Mom said.

"Oh God, can you just imagine?" Rachel said. "Somebody like me must have been kerosening her girlfriend's hair and accidentally lit a cigarette."

"Oh please." Mom said with a moan.

But a whole new list ran through my mind — a new gamut — the terrible scrapes Rachel might have gotten herself into, in her wild and provocative days. Accidents. A serious accident in which someone was killed. Getting drunk and hitting someone with her car. A hit-and-run. Blood on her bumper matching up in the forensic lab.

·   ·   ·

We moved a single bed downstairs for the beginning of the last week. On Thursday we were to take Mom, calmly, to the big hospital on the other side of the river. Calmly, because this was to be an operation, not a labor; and yet the idea had never seemed stranger than now. Like having a tumor removed. Benign or malignant, we wouldn't have a final prognosis until Thursday afternoon, when it would all be over.

Rachel said we were all to stop using the half bath downstairs except to go in and empty the wastebasket and put a hibiscus or a piece of fern in Mom's glass. In fact, Rachel took me aside Tuesday evening and gave me ten dollars to go down to the shopping center the next day to get a Monopoly set. My eyes widened at the extravagance, and she scolded me. "This isn't going to last much longer," she whispered, pressing the warm bill in my hand. "It can feel like the beginning. It can feel like the living end."

Could she have had abortions? I added it to my list, of course, but the idea did not leave me unforgiving.

At the big new mall my mind ran more to shoplifting.

Dad brought over a piece of plywood from the church, which he straddled on sawhorses so Mom could play Monopoly propped up in bed. He acted giddy as he read the directions on how much money to give us. It was the night before Mom's surgery. Rachel had absented herself, and none of us could concentrate well enough to remember the exact numbers of fives and tens, twenties and fifties, hundreds and five hundreds. We'd played Monopoly together many times, in Aunt Dove's cabin in North Carolina. Way before the change of life.

Mom with her old reservations kept saying, Goodness, it always sounded so complicated to her.

I sat scheming how I would get the secret out of Robin the next day at school if I took advantage of the fact that I had to be at the hospital at one. Robin might be moved to oblige me under circumstances such as these.

Meanwhile, Jeanie had begun reading aloud all the rules until Dad said we should just start or we'd be there all night.

Some time after eleven I got down to my last hundred. None of us could remember this happening before. Had anyone ever finished a night of Monopoly in the history of the game? We had to stop and read up on how I could mortgage myself and stay in a while longer.

Bankruptcy, I thought. One heard of people like Rachel, squandering their loved ones' savings; their parents' entire nest eggs; husbands' bonds cashed behind their backs. I remembered reading that compulsive gamblers stopped eating. For days they stood like heroin addicts, their faces blue from the light glowing inside the slot machines. They stood there until they were ruined, until someone had to lead them away. I marveled at how it was easier to forgive people such monstrous behavior than to forgive my own mother her most irritating mannerism.

"It's not right," she kept saying. It was making her uncomfortable to end up with the entire bank. Dad kept being sent to jail, where he would wait out his turn with encouraging groans of pleasure and regret as I continued, time after time, to land on my mother's property.

"Oh dear, I'm sorry, honey," she would say each time it happened, until I imagined someone rising up behind her bed to slug her over the head.

Suddenly, when the clock struck, we saw an unbelievable, surreal kick the baby made with its foot. The Monopoly set jumped like a Ouija board whose spirit has finally leaped out of darkness to spell something — the beginnings of a semiurgent message. Our pieces toppled. The Chance cards fell together in a heap.

"Oh, brother," Dad said, paling.

"I'll tell you, if you really have to know," Robin said.

I was going to be picked up right after lunch so that I could go with Dad and Jeanie; we all wanted to be there when the operation actually began. My worried face had worked on Robin, and she had, without much urging, decided to talk.

"It's just that your church hates my mother's guts. That's all."

I stopped chewing my sandwich. "Why?"

"Because," Robin said, "she was married to the dentist."

Robin hadn't rehearsed how she would say this. She stood up quietly and put her food inside her brown bag. She was suddenly very graceful on her feet.

"Wait," I said, "that's impossible. When?"

In those days no one ever talked about suing people.

That was surely lucky for Mom's doctor, who gave a little nick to the baby's head during the C-section, which is what we learned, finally, to call it.

It was a gash, in fact. Someone assisting the doctor had to put two little stitches above the baby's eye in her first five minutes. The surgeon had remained a little rattled over it, Mom told us later. It had been obvious to her the baby was okay, and she'd just lain there, watching his hands shake, wondering if she was maybe going to be one of the C-section moms to come out paralyzed.

Meanwhile we sat twiddling, in and out of anxiety — me and Jeanie and Dad and the only person who didn't have to be at work, Gwendolyn Helsor, gripping the sides of her chair. Each of us sat apart from the other, each alone so we wouldn't have to know who believed in praying and who didn't. Jeanie told me many years later she'd sat thinking she heard the lionesses.

But I could have thrown myself on the floor of the waiting room in my confusion. Just another Needy on our hands all this time? One of the real untouchables, her noisy jewelry and starched hair, and the extravagance of her, the hardness, the ridiculousness? How much more of a burden than a help she must have felt all this time. How awkward for my parents. She'd been down on the floor kneeling with the rest of them — night-and-day praying, with all the other followers, though I refused to think of her calling people up and quoting verses into the phone. But why not that too? I moved to a seat beside Dad in the waiting room to forestall the draining away of everything I'd felt for Rachel — all like so much sand in an hourglass; all of my love funneled down to the bottom half of myself. Had Dad always known, from the very beginning, that she was one of them?

Yes, he said. And he was surprised I hadn't been told. He was profoundly relieved, however, that this was all that was on my mind, since he was sitting there in that waiting room sweating blood.

"Was she trying to ruin you?" I said.

"No!"

"But Robin says everyone in the church hates her."

"Oh." My father sighed, exhausted. "Well, they did, I guess. It was hard for them to keep it up. Not after the dentist dropped her."

"Was he Robin's father?"

"The dentist? No, no. Women left men like Robin's father *for* the dentist."

"Well, what happened to him?"

"The father? Good question, poor man."

"Sir?" A nurse tapped Dad on the shoulder so that he almost fainted. "Would you like to see your baby?"

They'd secluded my sister Katherine for a few hours in an incubator as part of hospital policy for all C-section babies. Taken two weeks prematurely, she'd still managed eight pounds and stitches on her head while the real preemies lay on either side of her, motionless. They seemed barely to have bones. Some of them had panicky, fluttering chests. Like little pogy fish, Gwendolyn had sobbed, little slivers of nothing.

I couldn't turn around when Rachel Beale came up behind us. Rachel's hardest feature reflected in the nursery glass — her hair, always set in the same contours. I smelled the powder and cologne and listened to her subsiding tinkling sounds as she stood beside Dad and whispered she'd come as soon as the office closed.

"Caroline's in recovery," I heard Dad say. "The doctor told me everything's fine."

I didn't even turn around at the news that my mother was all right. I was afraid Rachel would instinctively reach out to me and hug me.

But the news that we were safe was expected all along.

Surgical disaster had been a distant threat after all. It struck people down, but we were not yet to be tested quite like that. A disease of swelling had tested my great-aunt Mary and made her faith strong, or so the story went. The tests I was set were so small, I failed them completely — the mere inability on my part to ever really appreciate Rachel Beale's narrow ankles again, or her raw frankness and weathered skin, all coming together in an absurd set of her misjudgments. All of them forgivable. But I kept seeing her floating up in the air like a feather shot up from someone's sitting hard on a pillow. The broad gestures of her fanning her toenails dry, humming a little over the pages of her magazines before thrusting a foot inside a tasteful, small sandal — something that dentist would have liked — one big toe squeezing out the end. Dear God.

"Was she really a member of his group?" I asked Robin finally, holding back the image of them, sweaty, and always always down on their knees.

"What do you think?" Robin said.

I could only shake my head and breathe deeply and keep wondering what in the world this made her mother *now*?

Luckily the baby had put an end to the baboon hour, and Rachel had left us in peace. But at school that day I felt drugged and tired. I wanted to go home. There was still English and Health to get through.

"Go ahead," Robin said softly, "ask whatever you want."

"I was just wondering what your mother is *now*," I said.

"What do you mean?"

"I just mean, if she's not a Methodist or part of the dentist's group anymore, what *is* she?"

"Oh!" Robin said. She understood my question, and I saw her struggle to give me the best answer she could. She really wanted to be my friend, to help me through this.

"I don't think she's *any*thing now," Robin said, looking to see if this made me happy. "She's never said, but I don't think she's anything now."

THE
KNEELING
BUS

THE LAST TIME I spoke to my father I had to shout. He was seventy-one.

"Did you see Bill Moyers on TV last night? Did you hear him interview those Methodist missionaries down in Nicaragua?" I waited for him to turn up the amplifying device on his new telephone.

"Yes," he said, calling back into the distance, "what about it?"

"Well, weren't you proud when they spoke out against the contras?"

He didn't answer. "Dad, can you hear me?"

"Yes," he said. "That youngest boy who did all the talking, you know who that was, don't you?"

"No, who?"

"Lauback's oldest grandson. The one your age. I thought you recognized him; I thought that's why you were calling up."

There is fame in the smallest circles, if you know enough: Frank Lauback invented the famous reading program "Each One Teach One."

My father wanted to talk about the weather in New York. He needed to know before he went shopping for the trip. "I'm coming up in two weeks," he said, "ready or not."

But we were not ready. Not my father; not my mother; not my sisters nor I. There was little warning — only a simple hemorrhage, we were told later — just enough life's blood to suffuse his brain one morning like a brief Methodist prayer, and he was gone.

At the time, I was teaching college English in Oneonta, New York, in the habit of spending my summers in Manhattan; long since out of the habit of attending church. But one summer a few years after my father's death, I took a sublet in Greenwich Village, and suddenly I kept coming upon Protestant churches when I was least prepared. There were so many of them in the neighborhood. They were very quiet for stone, for brick. I'd be on top of one before I'd see it, looming, between two brownstone houses, the narrow slip of sidewalk taking me by so close, I could actually reach out and touch the modest façade.

One Sunday I walked into a large, open church off Washington Square and found it empty at eleven in the morning. When I met the pastor by accident, he explained that his ministry was now, for the most part, a space ministry.

"A space ministry?" I asked. The man looked quite sane, but this was a city with a number of cults.

"You can see it's a big plant," he explained. "We invite organizations to use our facilities on a regular basis — a drug information center, the AA. Those kinds of programs."

"A *space* ministry!" I said, realizing that he meant space as in *rental* space. Poor man, what he really meant was that he had no congregation left. He had rooms. Rooms had become his church work now — freely given, but largely empty.

At first I didn't know how to take my leave of him; he seemed content to stand in the narthex while I looked around. The tremendous expanse of the sanctuary suggested much more space than I could actually see — underneath us, behind us, and on the other side of the plain white walls. A text came into my head: "In my father's house there are many mansions."

"Yes, indeed," he said and nodded. The idea had occurred to him, too, and he was grateful to me for having the background for it. He politely refrained from asking what it was I *did* in the world, although he couldn't help smiling as he looked me over. I was six feet tall and I looked like a forty-year-old spinster. As it happened, I was quite respectable — two marriages and serious relationships sometimes available to me. I was not quite out of the running, although he might have been able to tell that at one time I'd paused at crossroads.

Just before I left home. I was trying to make up my mind about college, and I used to sit in my high school library and read the bulletins put out by the five great Methodist universities that rhymed: "Emory, Duke, and Drew / Northwestern and SMU."

At the time, girls thinking seriously of the mission field

were encouraged to take degrees in Christian Ed. Sometimes the application forms for these programs would slip out and land in my lap and then slide to the floor to lodge themselves in my schoolbooks. In my bed at night I would ponder each essay question, one or two holding me in thrall for months: What is the work of the Living Church? I kept a secret folder of my answers. I never showed them around — not through college or the complications of the civil rights movement or the war in Vietnam or so many years of graduate school that I came out on the other side — grown, gone, and seriously counted.

The gold foil ceiling of the Washington Square church vaulted to fifty feet or more. The minister watched me looking up at the dome, admiring the restoration, which had been done with matching funds from the state. This was a historic monument, he explained.

I told him good-bye, noting how his hands were so like I remembered my own father's — the unusually tapered fingers, the large, graceful bones. Endangered species. At the Museum of Natural History right uptown, one could stand inside a special exhibition of enormous ribs, rigged together with invisible steel pins. The effect in both places was that of being cast back to a time when large herbivores held gentle sway.

My mother was due to come see me later that summer, and I had been receiving weekly reports from my younger sister, Katherine. Mom, she said, was beginning to show the strain. What Katherine meant was the strain of her inheritance, a belated and bewildering legacy from Aunt Dove.

No one ever guessed Aunt Dove had had an eye on us, or that the property she left our mother was anything other than an old place we called Camp. The most we knew of Camp was from a yellowing map hanging on her study wall — a long crooked finger of old hunting land through which ran Florida's Hatchineha River. "All set about with fever trees," she liked to say. Once as a whole family we had hiked in there with Uncle Wes, each of us wearing a veil of mosquito netting sewn to the beak of a man's oily hunting cap.

The birth of Katherine had accidentally caused a long delay in the legacy; a codicil from Aunt Dove stated that all my mother's children must be of age when the will was read. Aunt Dove meant to be out of the way a few years before the bequest was known. She hadn't thought there'd be a third child to hold up the inheritance for decades — for Mom to be old enough to be shocked, the sudden death of a husband far less shocking, in fact, than her sudden wealth. Years after the second tragedy and she was still not sure what she should be doing about it. Now Uncle Wes's Camp was standing at the back door of Disney World. When Jeanie's husband joked in passing that the government once bought the whole state of Florida for less than the land was worth now, Mom called me in a panic.

"Things are wildly out of kilter all over the country, Mom," I tried to reassure her. "Not just Florida. It's happening everywhere." I began to call her up before her visit with examples. "Did you read where a landmark church up here is negotiating to sell their air?"

"Their what?"

"You heard me. Just think of a church steeple and then

go straight up to heaven in your mind's eye. That's what they're selling. They have important air rights, and now they're letting it go."

"I don't understand," she said.

"Well, Mom, there's a large corporation that wants to put up a skyscraper behind the church. Sometimes a second party can have a say in these things. It's their ambience and it can't be ruined without compensation. That's what they're selling. Their ambience. For several million dollars."

I waited for her to say something. She didn't, so I added, "I expect the congregation will put the money to a lot of good."

Dead silence. She saw my point but didn't like my tone. She finally said, "I just called to find out what to pack for up there, if I'm coming. Is it hot or cold?"

It was a summer of family visits. At the last minute Jeanie decided to come, and she beat Mom to New York by two weeks. With her son Noel she flew in from Cincinnati, the two of them grinning in crisp new T-shirts. "You said not to dress up." Jeanie laughed. Little Noel was ten and looked exactly the way Jeanie had looked at that age, though not so fragile. He drew each breath in her same deeply thoughtful, wheezy way before he spoke. "No luggage." He shrugged, showing me his empty hands. "We're going to buy our clothes on the street."

Jeanie and I had become very close by telephone. She knew how desperate I was to bail myself out of Oneonta and move to New York. "Let's buy you an apartment!" she said. "Tell her Noel could come live with you here when he gets ready for college. Or who knows where

Kathy might want to end up? It could be a home for all of us. We don't have to be stuck in our little lives anymore." Jeanie was trying to be tactful. "There're more men here, surely," she added.

One slow afternoon near the end of their stay, I drove Jeanie and Noel across the Hudson to Drew University. Drew housed the documents and artifacts of Wesleyan history, the records of the whole Methodist Church. Jeanie wanted to show Noel his grandfather's name on a piece of microfiche.

The tiny museum was tucked away inside the Archives Building. They'd collected some chairs and clocks owned by the Wesleys and there were ceramic busts of John and Charles and oil portraits of Susanna Wesley, all looking quite severe. The relics would have bored my father, but we stood for some time before a painting of John Wesley on his horse — preaching to settlers and Indians — all of us in more danger than he could have guessed back then. Even little Noel was worried about the ozone. The idea of a whole planet steaming up and then evaporating, of New York and Cincinnati turning into Florida, and the temperature set on broil.

Noel especially liked a painting depicting five-year-old John Wesley being rescued from a house fire. *A Brand Plucked from the Burning* it was titled. "Why don't you bring Grandma to see this? She'd like it here," he said.

"I've got other things to show her," I told him.

"Like what?" he said, doubtful.

"Like an apartment," Jeanie murmured in my ear. "It might get the ball rolling."

"Why don't I just tell her I'm at crossroads in my life?"

"It won't work," Jeanie said. "Mom's very suspicious

of crossroads. In fact, I think she's completely against them."

According to Kathy, Mother had begun a course of serious reading. Books about Florida — its environment on the brink, its ecology out of whack, the fate of its wetlands in the hands of gangsters and state senators. Books from the local library had sparked her interest. She read regularly, anxiously, sitting at a sunny table too small for one person learning about inflation, the prime interest rate, and the national debt. She read: We are all living beyond our means and one day soon it is going to come down on us like an avalanche. "Now that's just the truth," she told Kathy.

Kathy called me up. "Isn't this just like Mom. Suffering all her life from lack of exposure and now her mind growing all potato root and lopsided. A ton of fertilizer at the last minute."

During the course of her visit I was supposed to come up with arguments to sway her; it was my turn to be firm. "Tough love" they called it in a book Kathy sent me. "You'll be doing her a favor," Kathy said.

Practicing my tough love in the morning had the effect of caffeine hitting my bloodstream: "Now don't think you can just pass that land on later when we're basically too old and set in our ways for it to do any good."

In bed, one shoulder and one hip up under the sheet, I would practice telling her, "Mom, if you sit on that land until you're ninety-nine, I swear I'm going to give my share to an animal home."

Once when I was five she'd discovered me sitting on the loveseat with my feet in an empty paper sack. I told her I was bored and didn't know what to do with my-self. "Use your imagination!" she had said and stood look-ing down at me with scorn until I went to my room and tied myself up with a cord, lost in some attic like the little girl I'd heard about who'd finally been found and taken away from her mother and given a whole different way of life.

It was her preference to bring up the subject of her valuable land. She liked to say it was easier for a camel to go through the eye of a needle than for a poor lady to figure out the right thing to do. "For example," she said, a weak line crackling late at night, "only the other day I was ap-proached by Florida conservationists."

"Who? Who did you say?"

"There's not much land down here now, Carrie, and the conservationists have their point of view just like every-body else."

"Mom?"

"What, honey?"

"I think I have to hang up now."

I'd thought about that camel all my life. I'd thought about it lately (now that my two humps, love and work, were starting to slump in different directions, the gristle in them shot to pieces); and I'd thought of it at a younger age, too, when the camel had been a lively text on which my father sometimes preached. Did the text really mean a camel couldn't ever get through the eye of a needle? he once asked. His congregation sat and waited. Well, he wasn't sure it did mean that. Modern archeologists had discovered that there was a gate in the north section of the old Jerusalem wall unlike any other, and it was called the Needle's Eye. Apparently it was so narrow, camels had to be stripped down in order to get through. So it was not impossible for a camel to go through a needle's eye. It just couldn't be loaded with riches the way they used to load them up in those days.

And when we'd sung the last hymn and my father had walked around the altar rail to lift his voice with us in the Doxology, I'd stood there, quietly, solving the problem in my mind. I'd been little Noel's age. If *I* was that rich man with too many riches on my camel, I'd simply strip him down outside the gate and send him on in naked. Then I'd carry in my loot myself, a little at a time.

Of course we all encouraged Mom to fly to New York for her visit. I was not surprised, however, to learn she'd wangled a ride up from a retired Methodist minister and his wife, people she barely knew. Reverend Canten was attending a Board of Missions conference on Riverside Drive, and his wife, Trudy, could use Mom's company during the business meetings he had to attend. But Mom would still have plenty of time to see her daughter in Greenwich Village. On the way home they'd all go through Pennsylvania and visit the Amish people.

I met Mom and Trudy in the lobby of the Hyatt. This moment was to be the best thing about the trip: me strolling in, higher than a chandelier, to carry Mom off for two days. Whatever I said in those ten minutes, whatever it was my mother felt — her pride flapping like a flag of forbearance — that was her reward for having gone to all the worry and expense of getting herself to New York.

Reverend Canten, it turned out, was a big braggart and

had almost ruined the trip. But not Trudy, said my mother, whispering during the cab ride downtown. "She's just a lovely girl."

Mom had tied on a plastic rain hat for the journey and seemed glad to keep it on for the slow crawl through midtown, where tons of steel and concrete rose over our heads. The rain hat was stenciled on both sides with silhouettes of girls in bouffant hairdos, and Mom, upon entering my dark sublet apartment, wore the hat on through another danger area: high shelves of books lined the long narrow hall. Friends of mine, trooping through the hall that summer, had admired the shelves, but my mother was too tired to admire, too far from home to get the beauty. She walked toward the light from the living room, her neck thrust out the collar of her car coat. When I'd gotten her settled with a cup of coffee, she confessed she'd felt any minute something was going to fall on her.

Late that first afternoon, she showed me a money belt she'd made to wear so she wouldn't be robbed when she was mugged. She'd found no one sold money belts in Florida, but a lady at her five-and-dime told her to use the bottom end of an old pillowslip. Mom had trimmed the pillowslip in soft upholstery piping. I watched her place two twenties inside before she retied the whole thing around her middle, where it disappeared, like a Saturday night special, under her overblouse.

"I'll be glad to give you this when I go home," she said.

"Well thanks," I said. "It reminds me, I have to stop at a cash machine while we're out."

She thought I was making a joke. The automatic tellers were still new to her; she hadn't seen one yet. I was watching her rummage around in her suitcase for another hat for me if it started to drizzle.

"I won't need one, Mom."

I could feel her looking at me while she continued to search. For years she'd been trying to figure out how I got to be such a missionary type without ever leaving the continent. She knew the kind — bookish yet restless, back from the field without having been thoughtful enough to bring home any slides to show people.

With time my mother had grown more cheerful, more painfully delighted. Perhaps she was always a version of what she'd become, but never so relentlessly overjoyed. We both knew how one day together could make me start to feel homesick in my own apartment, the book by my bed looking like a Bible in a bad motel, the drapes unfamiliar, alien, and my mother brighter than a sunbeam. She and I missed the younger Caroline in her. The loss could sometimes lump in our throats like a fist.

"You get such problem hair," she said, still looking for the extra bonnets. She was completely dependent on them now, she said.

"I won't need one, Mom. We're just going up to the diner."

"Oh, here they are. I knew I packed them. What color do you want?"

At the diner I got her settled in a vinyl booth and ordered souvlaki for our supper. She liked the sound, and said it to herself until she had it. "Souvlaki. I read there were twenty different kinds of Indians up here at one time," she said.

"Yes," I told her, "but this is Greek."

"Oh," she said. "I see."

I spooned hummus on a piece of pita and handed it to her. "Try this, Mom. It's made from chickpeas."

"Oh," she said. She was hungry, she said. But then she studied me closely and decided she wasn't going to talk my ear off. "I can see you're tense."

"No, no. Let's talk."

Well, she knew how annoying she could be when she talked too much. She didn't want to turn into *that*. In fact, she said, she always tried to save up interesting stories that would be amusing when the tension flared up. She knew a lot about tension now.

I took her hand, enfolded it. "Mom, I'm fine and I'm real glad you're here. Tell me what you've saved up."

"It's this funny thing I heard when I was shopping to come up here. I went all the way to Macy's."

"Macy's!"

"It's a nice department store in Orlando. You'd like it. Orlando's really changing."

"Things sure change, don't they?"

"Goodness, yes."

She blinked and looked past me, trying not to let the thought of Dad spill over to my side of the booth. She'd been sitting right beside him when it happened, and she'd noticed nothing until he'd opened his cloudy eyes once and then sailed on through her.

"So what happened at Macy's?" I asked. I could tell she had a joke. She was very good at passing them off as real.

"Well, there was a Kissimmee girl behind the counter, and I asked her if those were the scarves they had advertised on sale. She said, 'Them's *them*!' And I didn't realize until later what 'Them's them' really is."

"What is it?"

"You, an English professor? You can't guess?"

"I give up."

"Well, think about it now: it's a two-word sentence with *three* grammatical errors in it."

In another life, with other opportunities, Mom would have been what? New York debutante mother? Park Avenue hostess? ("Them's them." She chuckled.) A witty advice columnist. Something like that. An enormous hit.

"Mom, that's very funny."

Her careful saving had made her eyes water. She pulled out a tissue from her pocketbook. "I thought so," she said.

She had always been a hit.

I looked at her sitting opposite me in her secret money belt with the soft piping securing it in a double bow. It occurred to me to reach out and take her hand again, so she'd look up from her plate and say, "Yes, honey, what is it?" the way she used to. If I could just tell her while she was there for a few days. Tell her, without scaring her, how important it was I do something besides teach and that no load of bricks would fall on top of me if I quit. For years she'd been accepting the hazards of my life — distance and divorce, more than average. I'd always lived thousands of miles from my attachments and rarely felt free to come home; I wrote things she wasn't expected to read and had friends she couldn't ever talk to. I suddenly wondered out loud if I might have ordered food she couldn't eat!

"Oh, no, honey, I like these chickpeas," she said. "They're interesting."

The next morning I slept like a drugged person. I didn't hear her get up.

"Quiet as a mouse," she said.

I lay listening to her faint noises coming from the corner where the sublet had its kitchen. It was her practice, in cracking raw eggs, to take time to scrape out the stubborn part, the clinging half teaspoon inside both shells she'd been making sure of all her life. Her clean savings of odorless egg whites would fill sterilized containers the size of dishpans.

"You needed your rest," she said. She looked out my window and down at Abingdon Square. I recalled her joking the night before that my square sure looked like a triangle to her.

"I've had a nice morning reading," she said, and she had a sudden, dreamier thought I'd heard before. "Oh my, if I could go back to college now, I know I'd get a whole lot more out of it than I did then. I was just a party girl."

"Mom, every time you start in on this story I have to hear about poor Audrey. Let's eat, and then I have things to show you."

She was already reciting Touchstone's famous line about poor Audrey: "'An ill-favored thing, sir, but mine own.'"

Audrey had been her one dramatic part, with nothing to the role except in how she was so fully loved. In 1936, a college teacher had turned the party girl around by giving her a speaking part, taking her seriously. She guessed I knew how to do that for people. It was a calling, she said.

There'd been times when I'd recited that Shakespeare with her, our heads thrown back as if we'd been drinking all afternoon. "'An ill-favored thing, sir,'" each pointing at the other, "'but mine own.'" I'd said it, lovingly, to husbands, Jeanie to little Noel, and Noel to his two aunts. My mother had put the thought to great use over the years, securing from her one memorable bit of higher education the whole secret of life.

"I'm going to take you out on foot this morning," I told her. I watched her getting six last drops from an empty carton of milk. She looked up pleased, happy — more grateful to *me* than to anything New York had to offer.

"Oh wonderful," she said, "a walking tour."

There was still time, I thought.

It was early enough on Saturday for the streets to be empty. I wanted to stroll her past the storefronts I liked along Bleecker — the parrot store and the exclusive nightgown shop and the coffee shop with the whole window red with amaretti cookie tins. I could make these boutiques as familiar to her as the ones she knew in Orlando if I used caution and kept her west of Seventh Avenue, where men sold jewelry on pieces of cardboard and the subway entrances smelled of urine.

I had her arm and was heading her toward West Fourth and Bank when she said that calling this a village was a little deceiving. It was the same in Florida, though. "Circus Village," she said, closing her eyes. "Tranquil Park."

"Two hundred years ago this neighborhood *was* a village, Mom, when everything else was down at the tip of the island."

"I see," she said, cautiously.

After a moment, I heard her sigh in contentment at getting up to New York after all the complicated arrangements. "Long Island," she said, looking around, beaming at it.

"Manhattan Island, Mom."

"Oh dear, Manhattan," she said. "It's all going to be too confusing for me."

"Not if you change that little habit of yours."

"What habit?" She dreaded habits very much.

"Insisting something is confusing which is actually simple to grasp and, conversely, taking rather difficult concepts and making them simple. It reminds me of flirtatiousness in coeds."

Mom blinked. "Half the time I don't know what you're talking about."

I shortened my camel stride to match her stork step. Looking down at her, I saw how she was determined to like this little village if I liked it so much. Born to be generous, she was attempting to stroll with an open mind. I was about to reach out and put my arm around her, but then it struck me that her chin was tilted up with polite tolerance of all the uncollected garbage. She looked as if she were having to push the sight out of her mind the way she might the beggars and flies of Calcutta. In a few moments she said that Greenwich Village was interesting and I had another bad rush. I should have had a second cup of coffee, I thought. I should have had children.

In fact my crossroads looked a little pathetic that morning. Hazy and pinkish from the heat.

"Oh, I almost forgot," she said.

Her pocketbook was a compartmental affair with long zippers going in opposite directions. "I have a little map Mr. Garcia gave me to bring up here. He's Cuban."

"Mama, don't tell his nationality. It's so infuriating when you do that."

"It is? I didn't realize," she said.

"Well, try to realize!"

"He's been wonderful to me."

"Who has?"

"Mr. Garcia! He's helping me."

"We've all been saying how we ought to come down and help you now."

"Oh, sweetheart, that's thoughtful, but how can you, with all *you* girls have to do?"

"Well, you can't go around getting just anyone's advice."

"Now if I'd said that about Mr. Garcia, you'd call it prejudice."

"Well, who in the world is he?"

"My guru." She winked.

But in the meantime she'd found his tourist map of Greenwich Village. I saw the attraction of it for her — a triptych affair that gave a lot of information at a glance.

"Mom," I began.

"You take this, honey, and show me where I am."

"You're right here." I placed her finger on the corner of Bleecker and Perry. "Mom, we need to talk about this."

But Mr. Garcia's map was suddenly doing much more than I'd done to convince her that the Village was quaint after all. She had a view now. A little grid of streets on a solid green field, although what touched her most, she said, looking at me, was the wonderful fact of my living here.

She reached up and patted my face.

"Well, the truth is, Mom, I don't live here. It's one of the things I want to talk about."

She had heard my voice crack, and she reached up again to put a tuft of hair behind my ear. "It's been a nice change for you," she murmured, "coming here for the vacation.

You know how to get a whole lot out of something like this."

"Things aren't like summer camp, Mom. I'm middle-aged."

"I can't see it," she said, smiling, stepping back, nothing but admiration for me.

"And I've been thinking I'd get a whole lot out of something more permanent than my vacations."

"Isn't it wonderful you're permanent? And me saying all those years you'd get it." She did the same thing to the other side of my face and then had another, harder look at me now that I had tenure. She'd been waiting for it to make a difference. Like plastic surgery.

I tried to keep from giving in to a familiar sinking feeling. I was supposed to be steering her to the brownstone on Bank Street. It had a vanishing kind of beauty I wanted to have her see in the morning light: an antique brick wall in the living room, and her able to see from the sidewalk the polished floor and tracklighting throwing halogen spots on a few paintings.

Canvases hanging on a brick wall.

"Mom," I began.

"What is it, honey? What's the matter?" she said, looking up from her map. "Are you all right?"

"I've never kidded myself too much, have I?"

"Oh no," she said without pause, "you set your goals way too high, I always thought, and then went right out and achieved them."

I felt this praise leave her lips and poke me in the ribs of my bad faith. All my achievements. Only I knew what I was really like in that hour when I became the fly on the wall in my own apartment and watched myself watch Bill Moyers talking to those missionaries down in Nicaragua, all younger than I and more knowledgeable. Firsthand, stripped-down people, doing what they did in two languages and knowing how little time there was and that people were naked and hungry and in prison.

Mom was looking down at her little map. She was so genteel, she may simply have been letting me have whatever emotional swells I was having in private.

Maybe I should just go live with her, I thought. Just go live with her and find the time I needed if I was so serious about everything. It would take no money at all to do that! No apartment, no land sales, no desperate kicks to get an old lady off the dime. Whoever said one ought to make another person do anything? About anything!

Suddenly she spoke up and I was amazed to learn that Mr. Garcia's map could read my mind. According to this, Mom said, we'd soon come to the street where Edna St. Vincent Millay once lived in a house with her mother and, after that, the street where Marianne Moore once lived in a house with *her* mother.

"It's not far!" she said.

"All right," I said, thinking, No-nonsense women have often gone home so they can be productive and creative and not have to teach school . . . their mothers almost always outliving them.

"What's the matter?" I said.

She had looked up, startled. Did I realize we could go see the original café where Tom Paine wrote *Common Sense*? She had no idea things here were that old, she said. "I'm so ignorant."

"Mom?" I began.

"How did they save it all these years?" she said.

"Mama!"

"What, honey?"

"Can I just ask you something?"

"Of course."

"Are you ever going to sell any of that land while I'm still young? Some time in this century, by any chance?" The crack of hopelessness in my voice was like the first warning sound of an avalanche. Something bad was going to fall right on top of us both. "I just need to know," I warned her.

She folded up her map cautiously. "There are things you wanted to show me," she said. "I didn't mean to take over and be bossy."

"Oh, but I want you to, Mom." My eyes had watered over completely. (It would take a real artist to live with one's mother! A teacher wouldn't last five minutes!)

"Honey, you're not feeling well. I didn't realize it. Do you want to sit down?" She began looking around her. "Let's find a place to sit down and after we rest you can show me what you wanted to show me."

"Just that," I tried to say and pointed.

Her eyes followed the whole length of my arm and on across the street. She was determined to spare me the embarrassment of my welled-up emotions. After all, she'd had them herself ever since Dad died. She looked straight ahead and nodded at the building. "Who lived *there*?"

"Just try to concentrate on what I'm about to tell you. All right?"

"All right," she said, squinting, using all her concentration as if I'd finally plunked her down in my senior seminar.

"Mom, we could have an apartment in one of these beautiful buildings if you're prepared to realize what's happened to us. Aunt Dove's land could change our lives. Not drastically, but simply."

She was silent a moment. "Which one, honey? That one over there?" Her neck craned forward.

"Mom, I want us to buy some of that building."

"How much does it cost?"

"It costs money!"

"But you live a hundred miles from here."

"Two hundred miles from here! Just pay attention. In a few years, little Noel could come visit me here, or even live with me. Jeanie might be able to send him to Columbia instead of Ohio State. Kathy could do her post-whatever in New York. You could come stay with us. You'd be queen of this block. It's a miracle, what's happened to us. None of us has to be stuck in our little lives anymore."

She squinted at what must have looked to her like dirty red façades, one connected to the next and to the next, to the end of the block, and all the windows barred to keep out the drug addicts. "Noel here, honey? Why would you want to bring him here?" She was genuinely alarmed at the thought.

"Not now! Later. Do you know you'd have to go to Paris to find something this lovely?"

She patted my arm. "And when *are* you going to take a summer and go see Paris?"

"Mom, some of the world's great artists have lived here, according to your own map. And look. Look at these trees." I picked a leaf from over her head and handed it to her, suddenly remembering my first husband, an amateur botanist, explaining to me how these trees were very primitive on the evolutionary chain and should be extinct by now. "Ginkgo," I told her, closing my eyes against the vertigo.

"You mean that's the *name* of it?" she said.

"From China."

"I see," she said. I opened my eyes and watched, helpless, as she studied the ginkgo leaf on both sides. She'd been half expecting me to take her to a museum in New York. The expression on her unlined face grew solemn, responsible — as if she'd been asked to examine an artifact from the Third Dynasty. I was finally forced to reach over, take the leaf out of her hand, and fling it into the street.

"What's the matter now?" she said.

I shook my head.

"Well, honey, I've always known you liked trees. But you can't tell me the ones up at the college aren't as nice."

"Mom." I was sobbing.

"You're pale! Let's sit down." Then she suddenly let out a little cry. "Where are the benches?" she said. There was polite outrage in her voice. "Don't they have any at all?"

"Benches, Mom? Will you try to remember this is a city with eight million people?"

"Eight million?" she murmured. "No wonder."

No wonder? I began to raise my voice. Did she realize New York was something she'd never be able to fathom, even with all the assets she had, which anyone here could parlay into something wonderful instead of sitting on it, too frightened to move?

"I'm not frightened," she said. She still thought we were

having a reasonable discussion, but her jaw had dropped open at the sight of me angrily walking over to a cash machine and shoving a plastic card into the side of a building and pulling visible twenty-dollar bills out of a metal slot right in front of everyone on the street.

What was I doing now? she wanted to know. Didn't I realize that they could be standing over to the side watching me? They could follow me home to that apartment.

"Who, Mom? The poor people?"

"Well, honey, I don't mean they're *bad* people."

"You don't?"

"No."

"What do you mean? That I should be scared of them? You may as well know I can think of a certain woman, and I won't say poor — or halt or maimed or palsied — who might rob me much more seriously if she sits around much longer."

For a moment her mouth came open. Then she closed it, and I could have bitten my own tongue, except that she had already turned away and come face to face with an ad showing a woman posed in a pair of men's underpants. She could not figure it out.

"I know I'm behind the times," she said. "I've been seeing how far. Mr. Garcia says Disney's not buying now. It's all developers from California. We're getting three more amusement parks this year alone. You'd better not read what that's doing to our water table if you don't want your hair raised." She squared her small shoulders. "I don't know what I'm going to do. There aren't any quail left. They can count the eagles on one hand now." Then she started forward. I saw her pulling herself, instinctively, to the inside of the sidewalk, hugging buildings. Pointed south, she could see the beginnings of SoHo, where promising gallery flags flapped like bright blazes on some last great nature trail.

The M-5 bus could have been any bus in the world, for all my mother knew. She was simply grateful to see anything at all trumpet to a stop. She did not realize she had leaned against a pole with a bus stop sign above her head. Doors, it seemed, folded open in answer to some little prayer for guidance. I approached in time to hear her tell the driver she needed a place to sit down.

"And there aren't any benches," she explained, her voice trembling to break my heart.

"Mom," I whispered. "Wait."

But she kept pulling her arm free, wanting to escape me, and I couldn't even help her come up with the exact change she would have to have to board a New York bus. I had only the new twenties in the tight pocket of my jeans and a stiff money card cutting into my thigh.

"What's the problem, ladies?" the young driver called. "You need help getting on?"

My mother looked up at him, bewildered. "Of course not," she said. Then she rummaged around in her bag for a tissue.

"Wait a minute," he called.

These special buses were new to me. I had yet to see one perform the stunts they could do. This one seemed suddenly to tip on its side all along the curb line, and in moments the thing was poised to roll over on my mother. The noise was so unexpected, the side of the bus so massive, I felt my legs weaken and I couldn't get my mouth open to stop her before it was too late. I looked again and she had already disappeared. The bus was still falling, my own mother vanishing, unwarned.

"We have these in Orlando, too," a brave voice told the driver. She finally came into my view again, her little strained neck, at the driver's shoulder, bending so that she could see what was holding me up. "Come on, honey!" she called. Then the bus began to right itself and I was carried up on a ride.

"This is my daughter," she explained.

The young driver nodded, gave a seasick smile, and watched Mom thrust a handful of quarters at me. She must have been saving them up for months. She said she'd read quite a bit about how these buses worked on hydraulic lifts, and even as she spoke I felt a leveling-out under my feet.

But she was still too hurt to look at me. I stood and waited while she chose a seat to suit her. Near the driver.

"Where are we going?" I whispered. My poor mother was having to swallow her feelings before they ripped her to pieces. She pointed to the sign above the driver's head. It did not say that this bus was equipped for disabled people; no such euphemism. Instead, someone had cajoled the Port Authority into a rare act of naming: THIS IS A KNEELING BUS.

I would not have thought to describe it that way. I read the sign and envisioned a large humble elephant, of forgiveness and servitude, acting out its awkward obeisance. This despite the prompt thought that elephants had not roamed these parts in five million years! But I saw them nevertheless, getting ready to lift us all up, wincing a little out of stiffness, but getting ready, in different parts of

Manhattan — that simple gesture which would never cease to be my biggest embarrassment. And here were legions of them, each at a due moment, kneeling on just the one thick, tree-trunk leg with its improbable give at the knee, and that other old familiar trunk swung so easily aloft to trumpet and announce the trick of prayer.

"Do you enjoy driving one of these?" Mama called to the young man. "Is it more interesting than a regular bus?"

We were the only ones inside its hollow belly. My mother had pitched her voice to full volume to cheer us up. At first the young man acted as if he'd had enough of her and said nothing.

When he had to stop for a red light, he turned around, too friendly, his arm thrown casually over the back of his seat. "As a matter of fact," he called out, "now that you mention it, they're a lot more interesting than the regular ones, let me tell you! A man got on the other day without any arms or legs. He came on this bus head first!"

"Well, that's not what I meant," she said.

"Lady, it can't *help* but be more interesting, right?"

Wrong. My mother never allowed this kind of talk. I felt a rustling at my side as she smoothed her skirt and stiffened her back. Her fingers grazed my wrist and settled around the balled fist in my lap. Then she closed down on the driver like a steel door closing down on a dungeon — that loud clang — the echoes enduring for several beats. The young man chuckled and motioned to me to take a quick look. I had to lean forward and turn in my seat to see anything of her at all. My mother had shut her eyes. Her indignant brows had shot up and her proud mouth had pulled down. Around her too-small head her problem hair had fanned out. It was catching the light and spinning a halo she didn't know the half of — the individual strands having grown so thin and suddenly wondrous. She was lit up from the inside by her late sunbeam personality and any day now she was going to scoot on through that gate. She was going to scoot on through, leaving me here on the other side, loaded down and damned if I knew what in the world I was going to do before I had to strip right down to the bone and follow on after her.